The

This is a work of fiction. Names, characters, places and incidents are the product of the author's imagination or are used fictiously, and any resemblance to actual persons living or dead, business establishments, events, or locales, is entirely coincidental.

Blaze

COPYRIGHT is held by each author of her story.© Maya Blake, Sally Clements, Catherine Coles, Kat French, Tara Pammi, Suzanna Ross, Romy Sommer, Lorraine Wilson, 2012.

All rights reserved. No part of this book may be used or reproduced in any manner whatsoever without written permission of the authors, except in the case of brief quotations embedded in critical articles or reviews.

This book is sold subject to the conditions that it shall not, by way of trade or otherwise, be lent, hired out, or otherwise circulated without the author's prior consent in any form of binding or cover other than that in which it is published and without a similar condition including this condition being imposed on the subsequent purchaser.

ISBN-13: 978-1492770305
ISBN-10: 1492770302

Blaze features eight scorching tales by
The Minxes of Romance:

Maya Blake
Sally Clements
Catherine Coles
Kat French
Tara Pammi
Suzanna Ross
Romy Sommer
Lorraine Wilson

The tiny village of Coombethwaite in the English Lake District is the setting for the stories in Blaze, the first anthology from The Minxes of Romance. Romance is in the air for Coombethwaite's retained firefighters, and none of them will escape its heat unscorched!

To find out more about The Minxes, visit their blog,
http://minxesofromance.blogspot.com

Contents:
Memory's Flame by Maya Blake
The Fire Inside by Romy Sommer
A Smouldering Attraction by Suzanna Ross
Locked Into Love by Catherine Coles
Hot, Bothered and Bewitched by Kat French
Lighting Love's Spark by Sally Clements
Worth the Risk by Tara Pammi
A Kindling Romance by Lorraine Wilson

Memory's Flame

Maya Blake

Chapter One

She was back in Coombethwaite.

Seven days away from the Big 3-0 and her life had come full circle. Ellie Cochran glanced out the window of her late grandfather's three hundred year old stone cottage to make sure no one was watching.

Coombethwaite, Northwest England —population eight hundred.

Enough souls to ensure there was always gossip to go around. And yet, growing up here, it'd seemed as if she had been the sole grist for the village's gossip mill.

Even after she'd left. Especially after she'd left if her grandfather's gruff reports had been anything to go by. Apparently, her weekly film critic column in the nation's top newspaper was enough to keep the village residents in full tittle-tattle flow.

She pulled a light cotton shirt over her tank top and buttoned it up. Over her fair hair she tugged Grandpa's old beanie and settled it low on her forehead. If it had been daylight instead of a cool June night, she'd have added a pair of shades to complete the camouflage.

A mocking voice asked why she bothered.

Grandpa's funeral had been very well attended yesterday. By now everyone knew she was back. The rumour mill was working overtime.

But the frantic need to get away from the cottage for just a little while stormed through her. She checked one last time to make sure the oven setting was right for the small casserole she'd shoved in there fifteen minutes ago. Pulling open the door, she cast a glance up and down the quiet street, and stepped out.

In exactly seven days, she'd be gone. Tomorrow, she had an appointment with the estate agent in the morning, then the plumber and electrician in the afternoon. She needed the work to Grandpa's cottage done ASAP. She was prepared to pay through the nose for *ASAP* because the need to be gone from here was worth going broke over. Not that she was near bankruptcy. Her success at her job ensured she was comfortable.

Her job.

Yet another thing Grandpa had hated…

Up ahead, the glow of light brightened as the doors to the Rose and Crown Pub opened. Ellie darted into Coombe Street as several men spilled onto the street. Under the cloak of darkness she hesitated, her attention caught by the familiar build of one man. *Was it him?*

So far she'd been able to avoid him. And if there was a God above, she'd be able to keep a low enough profile to avoid running into—

He turned sharply, as if sensing her gaze.

Ellie jumped back further into the darkness, sucked in a breath and quickened her steps towards her destination. She didn't need to see if she'd been right.

According to Grandpa, Trouble had been her middle name.

But for the next seven days, she intended to avoid even the faintest whiff of it.

#

Jake turned back to his colleagues, the tingle in his nape abating with a roll of his shoulders. He was tired. If he'd had his way he'd have taken his pint sprawled on his sofa in front of his TV watching mindless drivel, not in the Rose and Crown with Ben watching his mates who weren't on call from the fire station playing the tired game of let's-out-drink-each-other.

But he'd been away for the past fortnight. And it seemed everyone wanted to know every last detail about the famous London Fire Brigade—right down to the colour of the Fire Chief's boxers!

Was it any wonder he imagined he was being watched from the shadows?

"Guys, I'm calling it a night." He needed a shave, a shower, and sleep, and not necessarily in that order.

Ben, his twin brother, eyed him with a smirk. "Don't tell me you're worn out from the bright lights in the big city. You're getting soft in your old age, bro."

"I'm older than you by two minutes, not two years, so enough with the old. And you'd be worn out too if you had to listen to you bang on about nothing for three hours straight."

"At least tell me you got lucky in London. Or made an attempt to engage a member of the opposite sex in any sort of *communication*?" His brother pleaded almost wearily.

For a second, Jake wanted to snarl that all guys weren't as lucky at pulling as his twin seemed to be. He barely stopped himself.

Deep down he knew the reason why. Even after all these years, he hated himself for the mental yardstick he attached to every potential relationship, where every woman was judged and found lacking. Sure, he'd indulged in the odd no-strings relationship, but every single one of them inevitably fizzled out.

He was so tired of the chase, there'd been no one in the last year; not since he turned thirty. More and more he'd begun to wonder if there ever would be. And the more he wondered, the more he hated himself for it.

"Are you sure you don't want to come back to mine to watch the footie?" Nick, his soon-to-be-married friend offered.

"No, thanks all the same. I'll catch up with you on Monday. Or if I'm called out before then." He was on call for the next forty-eight hours.

He shrugged off more 'light weight' jokes, stuffed his hands into the pockets of his lambs' wool jacket and struck out towards his house.

His footsteps slowed as he reached Coombe Street. Although the soft street lamps showed no one in sight, again his nape tingled. With stiffened shoulders, he quickened his steps past Mrs Cromaty's house before the nosy old gal stepped out to *casually* catch sight of him. He didn't feel like another good-natured interrogation, even though it would take a Spanish Inquisition to make him admit the stupid thing he'd done whilst in London.

He made it safely past her house and onto Prince Lane. With relief, he fished out his keys.

It'd barely scraped through the keyhole of his beloved barn conversion when the explosion ripped through the night air behind him.

Chapter Two

At first Ellie thought the sound was fireworks. From her crouched position at her grandfather's graveside, she looked up into the sky, and waited expectantly for the shower of coloured lights.

It never came. She held her breath, her heart climbing into her throat as the implication of what it could be sank in. Letting go of the flowers she'd been arranging over her grandfather's grave, she slowly rose, almost afraid to look down the hill towards Grandpa's cottage.

No…Dear God, please. No.

Faulty wires…not so sure about the gas connections either. The words of the surveyor filtered through her head. What were the chances…? Striding to the fence she'd scaled minutes ago, she clambered over it again, the old habit slipping back on like a favourite glove. Her landing wasn't as smooth as it'd been on the way into the graveyard and she felt a tear as she let go of the fence. Great, a pair of designer jeans, ruined.

From her position on the hill beside St Peter's Church, she saw the first signs of smoke and her heart climbed into her throat. She quickened her steps just as the faint sound of a fire engine's siren whistled through the air.

Please, please, please…

She rushed past Mrs Cromaty's and sure enough, the curtain twitched as the old woman went into full spy mode.

People were beginning to spill out onto the streets as she

broke into a run. The sight of flames licking up one side of her childhood home ripped a sob from her throat.

"No!"

Ellie didn't slow down. Flames and smoke spilled out of the back, where the kitchen was located. With any luck she'd be able to get in the front door and do something…anything, before the flames took proper hold.

Pulling the beanie off her head, she held it in front of her face, and lunged for the front door. Her fingers connected with the doorknob just as strong arms snagged her waist and yanked her away.

"I'm not sure whether you're stupid or plain crazy, or whether fires burn differently where you come from but there's no way I'm letting you enter a thatched cottage on fire, Ellie."

Shock ripped through her. She struggled to free herself. When the arms loosened, she turned and found herself face to face with Jake Spencer…her one time best friend. And the reason she'd left and stayed away from Coombethwaite.

#

Jake was thankful he didn't have time to dwell on the expressions criss-crossing Ellie Cochran's face.

Without stopping to think about it, he swung her into his arms and marched across the street, far beyond harm's reach just as Coombethwaite's single fire engine arrived.

"Stay here, and don't even think about going anywhere near that cottage."

Her lips—still bow-shaped and as tempting as hell, pursed. "But—"

"But nothing. Stay here and let me do my job, Ellie, or I'll get one of the other guys to come and physically restrain you." Over his shoulder, Ben and other members of the fire crew were already setting up the hose. The explosion had blown out the kitchen window and flames now licked dangerously close to the thatched roof. If it took hold, there would be no saving Cochran

Cottage.

"I'd forgotten how bossy you can get."

"I *haven't* forgotten how impetuous and hot-headed *you* can get. I can't worry about you pulling a fast one if I leave you alone, but if you want me to save your grandfather's cottage I need you to promise you'll stay here."

Her lips pursed further but the look she shot him contained a hint of sadness that tugged at him.

"I'll stay here. Go."

He nodded and released her. She caught his arm as he turned. "There's a box in the second bedroom…under the bed. If you can, please save it."

"I'll do my best. And, Ellie?"

"Yes?

"It's nice to see you."

Her lips lifted in a smile that didn't reach the sadness in her eyes.

"It's nice to see you, too." She glanced at the smoking cottage and her eyes darkened. The old protectiveness he'd always felt towards her pushed forward.

"Don't worry, I'll do my best. Do you have any idea how the fire started?"

"Casserole in the old gas oven. Or it could've been the wires. I think they're faulty."

"Okay." Pulling his helmet firmly onto his head, he bent forward and walked through the front door. Memories crowded in as he glanced around the small living room. He'd spent many stolen hours in here with Ellie when her grandfather had been away. Hours he'd mistakenly hoped would stretch into a lifetime.

Smoke flowed from under the kitchen door, which had thankfully been pulled shut. Jake breathed a sigh of relief. So far the fire seemed contained only to the kitchen but they had to act fast. Ben came up behind him with two canisters—one carbon dioxide, one water.

He glanced at his brother. "You yakked at me for three hours straight the minute I got off the train, but you couldn't find ten seconds to tell me she was back?"

Ben shrugged. "I figured you'd find out anyway. And frankly, I wanted to delay the return of *the look*."

Jake frowned. "What look?"

"The one you're wearing right now. The one that says I-don't-know-whether-to-scream-with-happiness-or-shoot-myself-in-the-head. Face it bro, Ellie always had that effect on you. I thought you deserved a good night's sleep before getting hit upside the head with that news. Of course, I should've known when she returned it would be with a bloody bang."

"Whatever you think of her, I don't believe Ellie is the type to deliberately get careless about fires."

Ben's jaw tightened. "Yeah, that's another reason I didn't tell you she was back. Even after twelve years, you still jump to her defence at every turn."

A bang on the door from the other side signalled it was safe to go in. Jake glared at his brother. "Maybe I wouldn't have to, if anyone gave her a chance."

He grabbed one canister from his brother, pulled off the nozzle tab and with a deep breath, headed towards the kitchen.

#

Ellie stood on the pavement, frozen despite the activity surging around her. She wasn't sure which part of the unfolding situation shocked her most – her burning cottage or the fact that she'd come face to face with Jake Spencer for the first time in twelve years.

The memory of him lifting and holding her close slowly fizzled through her, unfreezing her senses. A loud crash ripped through the air, galvanizing her forward. She was at the door when it opened. Jake filled the frame, blocking her way.

"What happened?" she demanded, trying to look over his shoulder.

"One of the kitchen cupboards fell down. The whole wall is seriously damaged but we managed to put the fire out before it touched the roof."

"Can I go in?"

He grabbed her arm and steered her back to the pavement. "No, we have to make sure everything's secure first."

"I have to—"

"Whatever you have to do can wait until the cottage is safe. I hope you're not thinking you can stay here tonight?"

She frowned. "If the damage is only in the kitchen, why can't I stay here after you've secured it?"

"The smell of smoke for a start. And there's no electricity and no gas. We've turned them both off as a safety precaution. As the explosion also damaged part of the water pipes, the kitchen's flooded, so there's no water either."

Ellie licked her lips as the words sank in. "So you're saying..."

"Until we declare the cottage safe and the fire inspector has been and approved any repairs, you can't stay here."

She closed her eyes as despair raked through her. So much for keeping a low profile and making a quick exit. "Dammit. Where am I going to go?" She wasn't aware she'd whispered the words aloud until Jake's hand tightened on her arm.

She glanced up to find his intent gaze on her face. He seemed to be gauging her reaction. The reason became clear seconds later.

"I have a spare room. You're coming to stay with me."

Chapter Three

Ellie sucked in a breath and immediately shook her head. "No, that's very generous of you but I can't. Thanks, anyway."

Jake's jaw clenched at how easily she'd dismissed him. The memories that intruded this time weren't fond ones. They were ones of Ellie walking away as if what they'd shared meant nothing to her. As if she wasn't trampling on his heart.

"Unless you're planning on camping in the park or sleeping on the village square bench, I'd take the offer if I were you."

"But there's no need. Coombethwaite Hotel—"

"Is fully booked. Nick is getting married next week. As of tomorrow, his fiancée's guests are arriving from all over the country for the pre-wedding shindigs they've planned. Even the motel and student's hostel are taken."

"But…won't your…wife object?"

His hand dropped. "If that's a subtle way of trying to find out if I'm married, the answer is no. No wife, no girlfriend. And I'll make sure my blow-up doll is well hidden." His attempt at a grin faded when her face remained serious. "That was a joke, by the way."

"Jake…"

He almost groaned at the never-quite-forgotten raspy sound of his name on her lips.

"What, are jokes forbidden in London these days?"

Her sigh blew the honey-coloured fringe off her forehead. The curls tumbling down her shoulders made his fingers itch to feel their softness again. He clenched his gloved hands into fists and kept them at his sides.

"Of course not. Just that..." She paused and looked around. Hastily averted gazes of curious residents made her lips firm before she stepped closer. "I don't want to set tongues wagging again, Jake. I really just wanted to bury my grandfather quietly, put his affairs in order and leave."

A chill swept through him. "So were you even going to look me up, or have you consigned me so far in your past I don't even warrant a hello? And since when do you care about people's opinion?"

She bit her lip. "You didn't come to Grandpa's funeral. I thought...you didn't..." She shrugged.

"I was out of town. I only got back earlier this evening."

Surprise lit her soft hazel eyes. "Oh."

"And about tongues wagging, I think you'll find they'll wag whether you want them to or not, especially if Mrs C is the ring leader. So you can either sleep on the bench, or stay with me."

She seemed to waver and the chill receded. He ignored the voice that warned him to be cautious.

Tugging off his gloves, he curled his hand over her arm. "Come on. I can't let you in on your own so I'll come with you to get your things, then we can head over to my place."

She blew out another sigh, the one he'd always associated with her capitulation. Deep down he felt a tiny hint of pleasure that *some* things hadn't changed.

"Okay...umm, are you sure I can stay with you?"

"I'm sure."

The remaining crew were coming out of the blackened kitchen as he escorted her in. Ben nodded a greeting at Ellie, then glancing at Jake's hand on her arm, his gaze cooled.

"I've updated Ellie on the damage and she knows she can't stay here. Is there any way to secure the kitchen? We don't want any teenagers to break in."

Ken Philips, the newest fire recruit spoke up. "I have a few plywood sheets left over from renovating my house. I can board up the windows with those if you like."

"That would be much appreciated," Ellie replied with a smile. "Please let me know how much it costs and I'll reimburse you."

Ken returned her smile, interest firing up in his eyes as his gaze wandered over her. "No, don't worry. I was going to throw them away anyway."

"That's very kind of you, thank you." She handed over her keys with another smile, and Jake had to bite back a growl.

"Off you go, then, Ken. Make sure you lock up tight when you're done." He steered Ellie towards the stairs, conscious of being the cynosure of several eyes.

Jake told himself he didn't care. Nope. Not one little bit.

#

Ten minutes later, Ellie sat in Jake's oak and granite styled kitchen. She took the mug of tea he held out and curled her chilled hands around the welcome heat. "Ben still doesn't like me."

Jake shrugged. "He's a grown man. Besides you didn't care what he thought of you when we were kids. Don't tell me you care now."

She glanced away and took a careful sip. "Childhood was a long time ago, Jake. In some ways it's easier not to care when you're young. I may not care what Ben thinks of me, but I'm not oblivious to the tension between you two when I'm around. Which was why I didn't want…" she waved her hand around his vast kitchen.

"He'll get over it." He brought his own mug to the centre isle and sat across from her. "So, how's—"

"How long—"

Jake waved her first.

"How long have you lived here? This place was just a crumbling old barn when I …twelve years ago." The conversion was stunning. Situated right at the end of Prince Lane on a slight incline, the large wooden-framed windows looked out onto Coombe Forest. It was too dark to see much, but the view would be spectacular in the day. Inside, the high beams and lovingly polished wood gave the whole space comfort and an enveloping warmth that just oozed home and hearth.

The perfect place to bring up a family…

"It was built eight years ago. I bought it from the previous owners three years ago when they decided to move closer to the Lakes."

"It's a lovely place."

"Thanks." Jake took sip of his tea, then leaned forward. "My turn. How's the big, bad cutthroat world of film critiquing?"

"I get to indulge my three passions – laying about, eating popcorn, and watching movies. Nothing cutthroat about it at all."

"Come on. Some of the two star ratings you give make my eyes water. I'm surprised there isn't a Hollywood hit-squad breaking down your door."

She glanced up in surprise. "You read my column?"

His gaze met hers in a frank assessment and the barest hint of challenge. "Why are you surprised? Just because you erased me out of your life when you left twelve years ago doesn't mean I've done the same."

"I didn't—"

"Yes, you did. You knew how I felt about you." He set his mug aside and the friendly neighbourhood fireman persona disappeared. "You've always known how I felt about you. I thought we had a future together. One minute you were in my arms, telling me how much you wanted me…wanted for us to be together. The next minute, you were boarding a train to London. I swore I'd never ask, but I've changed my mind, Ellie. I need to know why you left me."

Chapter Four

Ellie closed her eyes and tried to breathe past the rock of pain lodged in her chest. "Jake, don't do this."

She heard him move and knew the moment he stood at her side.

"Look at me, Ellie."

Reluctantly, she opened her eyes and turned in her seat. He'd discarded his heavy fireman jacket when they got to his house but he still wore the fire retardant trousers with the suspenders hooked over his powerful shoulders. She didn't want to feel attracted to the whole package, but heat nevertheless spiked through the pain and sadness welling inside her.

"I told myself a million times that what happened didn't matter; that you had a right to change your mind about us. We were both young and foolish, after all. But I've realised that it *does* matter. I need to know what happened, so I can move on."

Her belly somersaulted. "What do you mean *move on*?"

He shrugged, and her gaze was drawn once again to the wide shoulders underneath the black T-shirt. Her fingers tightened around her mug.

"It took me a long time to realise I was measuring every relationship against what we had twelve years ago. I'd start out wanting it to be just as perfect, then when it didn't turn out that way, I'd wonder if it was my fault…if I'd done anything to screw it up, the way I did with you."

The hurt in his voice touched deep inside her. "Jake, you can't live your life like that."

His laugh was full of bitterness. "Trust me, I know, which is why I want you to tell me. Did I screw us up? Did I do something to drive you away?"

She reached out and touched his arm, and tried not to react outwardly to the sensation of his warm muscles moving under her fingers. "No. It was never you. What drove me away started long before you and I became friends and eventually, lovers."

He frowned. "What was it, then? What was so bad you left and never returned?"

She swallowed, wanting to keep the secret she'd kept for so long from spilling out. But she owed Jake an explanation. She'd had no idea he felt so strongly about her leaving. Everyone else, her grandfather included, had been more than happy to see the back of her. To see the stain of the otherwise pure reputation of Coombethwaite Village removed once and for all.

"Ellie?"

"It was my mother, Jake. She turned up two weeks before my eighteenth birthday. She wanted me in her life. My grandfather told me I had to choose—him or her. I chose her."

#

Jake reeled under the shocking revelation. "Your mother? But I thought…didn't you tell me she'd died?"

Ellie nodded. "I thought she had. Turns out my grandfather made a deal with her. She was a struggling actress when she met my father. Some of the films she starred in were a bit…risqué. After he died, she couldn't cope with her career and me. She asked my grandfather for help. He didn't approve of her profession but with my father gone, he only had me. He told her the only way he'd help was if she gave me up."

"And she did?"

"I don't blame her. She honestly believed she was doing what was best. She had no idea Grandpa and I would clash from the day she left me with him. Or that I would end up being such a disappointment to him."

"I don't think you were…"

His heart twisted when the sad smile made a reappearance. "Of course I was. He told me that over and over again. He was expecting a biddable child. I had opinions, strong ones, which I was never afraid to act upon." She gave a bitter laugh. "I actually fooled myself into thinking it would change when I got older but he only got worse. By the time my mother turned up, the weight of his disappointment had become so crushing, I had no choice but to leave."

"You never said anything. Sure, I knew you were butting heads with the old man but all that time we were together, you never once said anything."

"Being with you was my only escape. When I was with you, I could leave my troubles behind, pretend everything was fine."

Her gaze slid away. Jake wanted to catch hold of her chin and tug it back to his. His hurt hadn't abated. Despite everything she'd said, he still felt a hole inside him. "You still could've told me all of this later. You could've written or called and explained all of it instead of letting me think I'd failed you somehow."

Her head bent forward and her shoulders slumped. "I know, and I'm sorry, Jake."

The hurt intensified. "That's it? *I'm sorry, Jake* is all I get?"

Her head jerked up. The thick lashes surrounding her beautiful eyes were damp with blinked back tears. But her face was set in determined lines meant to shut him out.

"That's all I have to say. You wanted to know what happened so you can move on. And I've explained." She stepped back from his grasp. He immediately berated himself for feeling the loss of her touch. "Now, if you don't mind, it's been a long, hellish day, and I'd really like to get some sleep."

Jake wanted to catch her back to him, to keep her talking until the tight band of pain around his chest was gone. But, looking down into her face, he saw the lines of strain and fatigue. Finding closure would have to wait a little while longer.

Gritting his teeth, he nodded. "I'll show you to your room."

The case she'd packed stood in the hallway. He picked it up and indicated she precede him up the stairs. The seductive shape of her pert backside told him he hadn't quite lost all brain-to-groin communication when it came to the opposite sex, unlike Ben's earlier allusion. By the time he showed her into the larger of the two guest bedrooms, he was thankful he still wore the lower half of his fire gear.

He set the case down at the bottom of the bed and watched Ellie turn around in full circle in the neatly decorated room. For the first time since he'd moved in, Jake looked at his house through another's eyes and felt a sense of pride in what he'd achieved.

"This looks really lovely, Jake." Her smile looked strained and he had the feeling she was trying to make amends for the abrupt end to their discussion. "In fact your whole house seems like the perfect place to bring up a family."

Pride was swiftly replaced by bitterness. "Funny, that was my intention too when I got this place. But I'm beginning to wonder if that'll ever happen. Sleep tight, Ellie."

#

Sleep tight. Yeah, right.

Ellie stifled a yawn and followed the fire inspector into the fire-damaged cottage two days later. Behind her, Jake lurked in brooding silence.

He'd been polite but distant since the first night at his house. He hadn't brought up the subject of their past and neither had she for fear of hurting him more than she already had. Her whole plan when she'd returned to bury her grandfather had been to let sleeping dogs lie.

Shame she had to go and cause a great big ruckus.

"So how long before I can get the workmen in?" she asked.

"The damage isn't as extensive as I thought, so they can start right away. None of the support beams have been affected, so the repairs should be pretty straightforward. I'll need to inspect after the wiring has been done and conduct a final inspection when everything's completed."

"I won't be here by the time it's all done, but I'll make sure the estate agent allows you access."

Jake gave a sharp intake of breath. Unable to resist, she glanced over her shoulder. Grey eyes bore into hers with an intensity that set her stomach fluttering.

She barely heard the rest of the inspector's words as he finished his report and left.

"So you're not even sticking around to see the repairs done?" Jake threw at her the moment they were alone.

"I have a job to return to, responsibilities to fulfil."

His hands fisted in his pockets. "Of course. And a guy whose bed you're missing, no doubt?"

"Is that your way of asking if I have a boyfriend?"

His jaw tightened. "Do you?"

"No, I don't." She tried to get past him. His hands shot out of his pockets and restrained her in the doorway to the kitchen.

"Let me go."

"Tell me what you meant by you won't be around when the works are done. How long exactly were you intending to stay?" His probing gaze demanded an answer.

"My return ticket is for Saturday. I'm needed at work on Monday."

He drew closer. His scent filled her nostrils, rushing to her head like a new and exhilarating drug.

"That's just five days from now. Christ, Ellie, if the fire hadn't happened, would you have looked me up at all?"

"Jake, please…"

"Tell me. I need to know that you'd have come to see me, just for old times' sake."

"The old times didn't end well for us, did they?"

His arms went around her and pulled her closer until her breasts touched his chest. Before she could stop herself, her hands slid around his shoulders.

"That depends on whether you choose to remember the bad times or the good times." His lips descended.

Ellie held her breath. "Jake…"

"Right now, I'm choosing to remember the good times."

His kiss shot fire straight through her. From the tips of her fingers to her toes, sensation engulfed her as Jake's tongue plunged into her mouth with forceful demand.

A groan echoed around the smoke-singed room. She wasn't sure whether it came from her or Jake. All she knew was the pleasure that washed over her, escalating until she felt liquid heat ooze between her thighs.

Jake cupped one breast in his hand as he propelled her back to trap her between the lintel and his hard-packed body. One hand plunged into her hair, stilling her for the further invasion of his mouth as his thumb teased her nipple. He swallowed her cry, his hips rocking into hers so she couldn't mistake the evidence of his arousal.

Her fingers dug into his shoulder and with every atom of her being, Ellie wanted to experience the magic she'd felt once upon a time with Jake. He tweaked her nipple once more. A shudder raked through her body.

Jake froze. Slowly, he lifted his head, his gaze locked onto hers. The only sound in the room was of their harsh breathing as they stared at each other.

"We were friends long before we became lovers, Ellie," Jake rasped. "I could seduce you into spending the next five days in my bed so we can relive the lovers' part of our history. But I don't think I can survive you walking away again if I let that happen."

"I don't want us to fight, Jake."

"I know you don't. Neither do I. Which is why I'm choosing

the friendship route." He dropped his hand from her breast and stepped away.

From the look in his eyes, Ellie had the feeling he was missing the contact just as much as she was. She licked her lips and forced herself not to reach for him. "What's your plan?"

He took a deep breath and started out of the cottage. "The wedding party are hiking up the Black Coombe tomorrow, followed by a barbeque at the King's Head in the evening. Would you like to come with me?"

The chance to spend time with Jake instead of wallowing in a well of regret was very welcome. She summoned a smile "I'd love to."

Chapter Five

"Keep up, slacker."

"Shut up. Just because you eat mountains for breakfast doesn't mean the rest of us feel inclined to rush up them at breakneck speed."

Jake laughed and slowed his pace to match hers. Up ahead, about twenty-five members of Nick and Lizzie's wedding party were making their way towards the halfway point of Coombethwaite's famous mountain.

"You don't really lie about all day watching films, do you?"

"I wish. Each film I review requires a huge amount of research so I spend most of my time hunched over a computer or on the phone to studio contacts. One wrong piece of information and I'm toast."

"But don't you also attend movie premieres and interview celebrities?"

Ellie grimaced. "After the first few red carpets, it gets a bit tedious to be honest. And aside from the rare celebrity, they're all as absorbed and diva-like as they try to pretend they're not."

Jake glanced her way when she sighed. "You sound like you're fed up with it all."

She shrugged. "Not fed up, exactly. I just wish I could do my job without all the extra baggage that comes with it. But in a place like London, you have to go with the flow or sink. What about you? I never thought you'd make a career out of playing fireman to my damsel in distress. You're very good at it by the way, Mr. Deputy Fire Chief." She bumped shoulders with him.

He grinned down at her, flashing white teeth in the early morning sun. Something tugged hard in her chest. Jake Spencer's dimples had always possessed the power to reduce her insides to putty. She tried to steel herself against them but found she couldn't look away.

"Hah, I loved it so much because back then, getting you to play dead was the only time I could get you to shut up."

He sidestepped the blow she aimed at his arm and laughed as she tripped over her feet. He righted her, the action bringing her flush against him. The effect of his hard, lean body knocked the breath from her lungs.

When his gaze dropped to her lips, Ellie held her breath.

An eternity later, he stepped away. "Come on, let's catch up to the rest."

Calling herself ten kinds of fool for getting caught up in what she had no business getting caught up in, she quickened her steps after him.

The rest of the day passed in a friendly, laughter-filled atmosphere. The couple-to-be were clearly besotted with each other, and many times Ellie had to curb the sharp pang of jealousy.

On occasion, she caught Ben's cool, speculative gaze but shrugged it off. It felt too good to reconnect with Jake again to let her mood be dampened.

The barbeque was winding down when Ben cornered her at the buffet table.

"So, when are you leaving?"

"Eager to see the back of me, Ben?"

"Eager to see to it that my brother's head doesn't get messed with again the way it was when you left the first time."

"A lot can happen in twelve years. I'm not the same person I was back then."

"Neither is Jake. He's not the eager sidekick who's content to get into mischief with you at the drop of a hat."

She glanced over to where Jake stood in conversation with one of the groom-to-be's sisters. He'd filled out so much more and in all the right places. Heat coursed through her and settled in her belly as her gaze lit on his formidable frame. Aside from the impressive body, he'd also developed a much more authoritative personality. Where he'd been attractive before, now he was downright *hot!*

"Yes, I can see that."

"I really hope you can. Because if you hurt him again, you'll have me to deal with this time."

He sauntered off, leaving acid churning in her stomach that quickly eroded her appetite. Abandoning her plate, she reached for the bottle of red and poured herself a glass instead. She'd taken her first sip when Jake sauntered up, pint in hand.

He peered down at her. "Are you okay? I saw Ben talking to you."

"I don't need rescuing, Jake. I can fight my own battles."

He glanced over at his brother, then back at her. "Dammit, Ellie. What the hell did he say to you?"

She took another gulp of her wine. "That I shouldn't mess with your head or he'll kick my ass…or something to that effect, anyway."

"I'll talk to him—"

"No, you won't. See, *this* was what I was trying to avoid."

"Barbecues on a warm summer evening with people who care about you?" His snarky tone didn't quite hide the hurt behind his words.

"No. Getting caught up in…in *issues.*"

"What *issues?*"

Unbidden tears clogged her throat. This had all been a mistake. Being around Jake, around his friends and family reminded her acutely of what she'd never had.

She slammed her empty glass down. "Never mind. I'm

heading back to the house now. Please thank your friends for me." She turned and darted towards the pub garden gates.

"Ellie, wait!"

The need to escape became paramount. She plunged through a group of men gathered around the exit and rushed into the street. She didn't stop running until she reached the pond opposite the Town Hall.

It was only as she slowed to catch her breath that she remembered she didn't have keys to Jake's house. The thought of returning to the barbeque made her insides churn faster. Skirting the pond, she approached the sole bench, and sat.

Looking down, she found and traced the ingrained X on the inside arm of the bench.

This had been their rendezvous spot, when they were sure the whole village was asleep. They'd smoked their first, and last – thank God – cigarette on this bench. They'd also shared their first kiss here.

Everywhere she looked, memories abounded. But unlike the suffocation she'd felt when she first arrived, she recalled the much happier times she'd spent here with Jake.

What the hell was she doing letting this place grow on her again? There was no way she and Jake would ever work. She'd never succeeded at forming a functional relationship…

Jake, with his perfect barn conversion, his perfect group of friends and his perfect job rescuing cottages from fires, deserved better than that.

Pain gripped her insides as her forefinger traced the wood one last time.

Firming her lips, she rose and walked the rest of the way to Jake's house.

He stood on the front step, his hands in his pockets, gaze fixed on her as she walked up the path.

"I don't like it when you run from me, Ellie."

She thrust both hands through her hair, unable to stem the

ever-rising flood of pain. "I lied to you, Jake."

He tensed. "When?"

"When I said I didn't leave because of you. I lied."

His indrawn hiss made her reach out to him. "No, don't get me wrong. My grandfather was the main reason I left. But he wasn't the sole reason. I could see a pattern emerging…people… *you* were beginning to form expectations. After that first time we made love, you were already picking out the white picket fence."

"I'm an old-fashioned guy. I want a wife and kids and a dog or two thrown in. I won't apologise for that."

"Don't you see? I never wanted you to have to apologise for it. But it wasn't what *I* wanted, not then. I couldn't find a way to tell you that without hurting you. But I never thought you'd blame yourself for me leaving. I'm sorry for that, Jake. Truly sorry."

He shrugged. "I'm made of tougher material than you give me credit for. I may not like it, but now I understand what made you run, I know to adjust my expectations accordingly."

She frowned. "What do you mean?"

He pulled his keys from his pocket and opened the door. "Come in, Ellie."

She followed him into the house and turned as he shut the door. "You're leaving in four days. I know there's nothing I can do or say to stop you. But we don't have to spend the whole time fighting." He reached out and caught her around the waist.

The impact and heat of being in contact with him stalled her breath. "Jake, what are—?"

He pressed a finger against her lips. "We've tried the friendship route. We nearly succeeded in going a whole day without fighting. Frankly, I think it's the words that get in the way." He took his finger away and replaced it with a light kiss. "Maybe it's time to try another tactic." His fingers dug into her waist and pulled her closer still. "If you agree, kiss me."

She was rising onto tiptoe before he'd finished speaking. Her lips met his in a heated melding that blew her clean away. After that, they let their bodies do the talking.

Jake released her mouth long enough to fling her fireman-style over her shoulder and carry her up to his room. In silence, they undressed one another, their sighs and groans speaking to a need that spanned many years.

Before long, she was sprawled on his king sized bed, Jake's lithe, solid body poised over hers.

His gaze swept down over her body in frank, heated appraisal. "You're even more beautiful than I remember," he rasped, and followed the compliment with a lingering caress over her breasts, wringing a soft cry from her when he grazed her sensitive nipples.

"And *you've* filled out in all the right places." Her fingers drifted over his pecs, down over solid six-pack to tease the skin just below his navel.

His breath caught and he leaned down and pressed a hard kiss on her mouth. Immediately, she became lost in sensation. They parted long enough for him to reach for a condom. His heartfelt groan as he entered her echoed her own. They found their own special rhythm, their breath catching and mingling as they embarked on an inevitable path.

Jake caught her to him as she shattered in his arms. A heartbeat later, he groaned his own release, the sound of her name on his lips causing her heart to contract sharply.

Ellie pushed the distressing feeling away. This was a time for pleasure, not the time to count the minutes until she would have to walk away from Jake one more time.

She felt his kiss against her forehead and relaxed into his body.

"What happened after you left with your mother?" he asked.

"We tried to connect, we really did. But she was set in her ways and I was set in mine. I stayed with her for about a year and a half, then I moved out. I got a job at the newspaper shortly after that, and worked my way up the ladder."

"Do you keep in touch with her at all?"

"Yes, we meet every month or so for lunch. We have a… relationship of sorts." She sighed and he gathered her close.

He kissed her again. "That's good. You better sleep now. I can't promise I won't wake you up as soon as I've recovered to have my way with you again."

She laughed, even as sleep blanketed her. As her eyes drifted shut, Ellie couldn't help but think…this was the most peaceful she'd felt in a long time.

Chapter Six

Jake scooped up the two cups of steaming coffee and headed back to his bedroom three mornings later. He was grateful he wasn't on call for another twenty-four hours.

But even if he'd been he'd have switched with one of the other guys.

Ellie was leaving tomorrow. His steps faltered on the landing and he stopped to suck in a deep breath.

No, he wasn't going to dwell on that. He'd promised to keep things light and breezy, and that was what he would do even if it killed him.

He entered his bedroom to find her propped in bed, her iPad in hand. The sheet covering her breasts slipped a notch and he nearly dropped the coffee. When she looked up and smiled, he knew he was in serious trouble.

He summoned an answering smile and handed over one mug. Then he reached into the top drawer of his tall boy and flung the DVD onto the bed.

She picked it up, her stunning hazel eyes widening. "You have a DVD of *The Notebook*?"

"You did a Christmas segment last year, naming your top ten favourite films. That was the top of the list."

"And so you bought it?"

"I wanted to see what the fuss was about."

"And?" she looked up at him.

He shrugged. "Frankly, I *still* don't know what the fuss is about. It's sappy, to say the least but…" Her raised hand stopped him.

"If you ever want to leave this room with your bits intact, I suggest you stop speaking right now."

He grinned, popped the DVD into the machine, shucked off his joggers and got back into bed. "I was going say *but*… I'm willing to watch it again with you in the hope that I might gain new perspective."

A look crossed her face that dared to give him hope even though he knew he was foolish to feel that way. He reached for the remote and pressed *play*.

Half an hour later, she gave up trying to explain what was happening on screen. Instead, he coaxed Ellie on top of him. Before long, her gasps of bliss filled the room, her head thrown back as she rode them both to ecstasy. When they both caught their breaths, he muted the TV and watched her fingers play over his chest.

"I never told you where I was when you came back to Coombethwaite."

She raised her gaze to his. "Where were you?"

"I was in London, attending a job interview at the LFB."

Ellie raised herself onto one elbow, astonishment in her eyes. "You're leaving the village?"

"Not for good. The Fire Brigade approached me last year to head up an exchange-training programme. I met up with them to see how to work things out." He played with a strand of her silky hair, then took another breath. "I looked you up when I was up there. I told myself I wouldn't, but I did."

"How did you know where I lived?"

"I didn't. I looked up the address of the newspaper where you work and I went to your office. When they told me you weren't there, I didn't believe them. I thought maybe you were deliberately avoiding me. I got annoyed and decided to camp out at the coffee shop across the street."

Her shocked laugh tingled down his spine. "*You did what?* For how long?"

"Let's just say it took several cups of double shot, non-sweet, half-fat machiattos or something equally disgusting to make me realise the receptionist was telling the truth after all. I went back to my hotel and topped off my misery with stupidly expensive mini-bar vodka and woke up with a hangover strong enough to knock Mrs C off her perch for a week."

She laughed and the sound filled up the dark, abandoned shadows of his soul. He wanted to keep cracking stupid jokes so he could keep listening to the sweet sound.

"You could've just picked up the phone and called, Jake. I'm listed in the phone book," she berated as she melted back into his arms.

As he lost himself in the kiss, Jake was glad he didn't have to confess that the sound of her voice wouldn't have been enough. That the need to see her, to be in her presence had been one he hadn't been able to deny himself.

A need he had a feeling would shatter his heart if he let himself dwell on the fact that in a little more than a day she would be gone again.

#

Ellie shut and locked the door to Cochran Cottage. She tucked the box of letters firmly under her arm to stop the light drizzle from damaging it.

Jake was at the fire station this morning. She'd taken the opportunity to finish her packing, so she could avoid further heartache.

She sucked in a breath as she recalled the look on his face as he'd left this morning. Ellie had no doubt that same look was reflected on her own face.

She was in love with Jake Spencer, had always been truth be told. But as her grandfather and her mother had widely demonstrated, love on its own was never enough. Relationships required more, and she didn't know whether she had *more* to give.

Tears prickled her eyes but she forced them back. She'd walked away once. She could do it again. She refused to look around the village as she made her way back to Jake's house.

Packing done, she sank onto the bed. She had a few hours to spare before the taxi arrived to take her to the train station. She wasn't even sure whether Jake would return or not.

She took out the letters she'd found when she'd gone through her grandfather's things. The first letter—a love letter full of longing and heartbreak for the woman he couldn't have—gave her the first glimpse into the hitherto hard man she'd thought her grandfather had been.

Tugging off her shoes, she made herself comfortable on the bed and unfolded the rest of the letters. Her quiet sobs as she read the final letters turned into hiccups as she hugged her pillow close and wept for what her grandfather had lost.

#

Ellie jerked awake, crying out in horror as she noted the long shadows. A quick glance at her watch had her launching off the bed. Grabbing her suitcase, she flew down the stairs.

The taillights of the taxi were disappearing as she pulled open the front door.

She rushed onto the road after it. "Hang on! Wait!"

At first she thought he hadn't seen her. Then the car rolled to a stop.

"Oh, thank you!"

She jumped in the taxi, carefully avoiding the driver's gaze. She was sure she looked a sight with her tear-streaked face and flat bed hair.

"Keswick Station, was it?"

"Yes, please." She swiped a hand over her face and was busy smoothing down her hair when she heard the driver's sharp exclamation.

She looked up. Jake's fire truck stood crossways over the

bridge.

He stood in front of the truck, his hands folded across his chest.

The driver stuck his head out. "Is there a problem, mate?"

"Yes. There is." He didn't elaborate, just stood there, his gaze locked on hers through the windshield.

The driver cleared this throat. "Err, miss, do you know what's going on here?"

Ellie licked her lips, her heart beating like a jackhammer. "I…I think so but I have to get out to find out."

"Listen, I'm not sticking around for this. I've already wasted half an hour waiting outside your house, I'm not—"

"It's okay. Here," she fished out several notes, passed them to him and got out. He slammed her door, muttering under his breath as he reversed his taxi.

Ellie barely heard what he said because Jake finally moved, his long, sure strides eating up the space between them until he towered over her.

"You said it was easier not to care when you're young. Does that mean you care now?"

The tears she'd been holding back clogged her throat. "Jake, packing my things today was the hardest thing I've done in a long time."

"Then don't go. God, I love you so much, Ellie. I've loved you for a long, *long* time. I don't think I'll survive if you leave me again. And if leaving again is as hard as you say, doesn't that tell you that you feel something for me too?"

"I can't…I can't stay here, Jake. Grandpa spent his whole life being disappointed in me. I think it's better for me to leave before I disappoint you too."

"You could never disappoint me. And don't judge your grandfather too harshly. Despite what you think, he was proud of you. He bragged to his cronies about what a success you'd made of your life."

"He did?"

"Yes." He eased the suitcase from her numb fingers and set it down. "Stay here. Let everyone see the success you've become. Then instead of being Cochran's wayward granddaughter, you can be Ellie Cochran, film critic extraordinaire. And…God willing…Jake Spencer's wife."

Her breath caught. "Jake…?"

He closed the distance between them and sank smoothly onto one knee. "Yes, Ellie. I am most definitely asking you to marry me."

"Oh my God!"

"Is that a yes? We can make this work, I promise. I'll take the training job in London and we can split our time between both places."

"It's an abso-fricken-lutely!" She sank down to join him on the ground, her heart alight with warmth. Placing her hands on his stubbled cheeks she kissed him soundly. "I love you too, Jake Spencer."

Words lost their meaning for a very long time after that. Eventually, she convinced Jake to move the fire truck – or risk being arrested by the local constabulary. As he was still on call, she elected to stay with him at the fire station until he came off duty.

Ben came in just before midnight. When they broke the news to him, he slapped his brother on the back in congratulations. He eyed Ellie speculatively for several moments, then nodded, as if satisfied with whatever he saw in her face.

"Welcome to the family. Sorry I gave you a hard time." He kissed her cheek.

Ellie smiled. "I would've done the same in your shoes."

He gave a cheeky salute and left. Strong arms tugged her close from behind. "Are we leaving now?" she asked.

Jake's stubble nuzzled her cheek, sending a frisson of electricity through her. "Not just yet. I have a surprise for you."

She turned in his arms. "Really?"

He nodded. "Come with me." He led her around the back of the fire truck and motioned her up the ladder.

She started in surprise. "You want me to climb to the top of the truck?"

He just smiled and waited. She climbed the rungs to the top and gasped at the sight before her. A single flame burned in a candle on a rug laid on the truck roof. A bottle of champagne stood in a silver bucket along with two glasses.

"What's this?" she breathed.

"It's your birthday in," he checked his watch, "fifteen minutes. I thought we'd start the celebration a little bit early with a little trip down memory lane." His fingers made easy work of her shirt buttons. "You once told me how you'd love to play hooky in a real fire truck."

Excitement fizzed through her. "Hmm, I remember. I'm surprised you do, too."

"My memories of us never dimmed. Not for a second. Happy birthday, Ellie."

She went into his arms, and knew she was finally home. "I'd love to make more memories with you, Jake. Enough to last a lifetime."

About the author:

Maya Blake fell in love with the world of the alpha male and the strong, aspirational heroine when she read her first romance novel at age 13. Shortly thereafter, the dream to plot a happy ending for her own characters was born. Maya lives in South East England with her husband and two kids. Reading is an absolute passion, but when she isn't lost in book, she likes to swim, cycle, travel and Tweet! You can get in touch via her blog: www.mayabauthor.blogspot.com
Twitter: www.twitter.com/mayablake
or Facebook: Maya Blake

Books By Maya

Hostage to Love
The Sinful Art of Revenge
Marriage Made of Secrets
The Price of Success

The Fire Inside

Romy Sommer

Chapter One

Ryan Morgan climbed out of his sports car and rested his arm on the roof for a moment as he surveyed the landscape, the clear sky above, and mountains reflected in the dark water of Coombethwaite Lake. He breathed in deeply.

For the first time since he'd left London, the tension in his neck and shoulders eased. With luck, the tension would be history by the end of tonight's stag party.

The King's Head pub sat on the very edge of the water, separated from the lake by nothing more than a slope of lawn scattered with wooden tables and benches, almost all occupied on this fine summer's evening. He shielded his eyes against the glare of sunlight off water. It was a moment before he spotted Nick.

His uni flatmate hadn't changed a bit in the years since they first met. He still wore his hair cropped short, and still had the physique of a man who worked out regularly. Ryan kept in shape, and knew he wasn't too shabby for a man in his mid-thirties who spent way too much time in an office, but beside Nick and his brawny mates, he no doubt appeared a lightweight. He slammed the car door shut, pocketed the key, and headed across the lawn to where Nick and his friends laughed loudly at some joke.

Nick looked up as he approached, and grinned. "Hey, you're late. Sam's inside getting us the next round, so you'll have to hurry to add yours to the order."

"Hey there to you too." Ryan laughed. Just being around Nick again made him feel years lighter. He headed inside, into the gloomy pub with its low-beamed ceilings and wallpaper the colour of dried blood. A couple of tables were occupied, but the only person being served at the bar was a young woman. No sign of Nick's mate Sam.

Ryan leaned against the dark wood bar and waited as the barman filled her order.

For half a second, the young woman glanced his way. He caught the interested flare in her eyes before she quickly looked away. She tucked back a stray wisp of hair that had fallen loose from her untidy ponytail, an unconscious gesture that made him smile.

"I'll be with you in a moment." The barman sent him an apologetic grin as he pushed two foaming pint glasses across the bar towards the young woman. "Here you go, Sam."

"You're Sam?" He couldn't keep the incredulity out of his voice.

She turned, hand on hip, stance shrieking defiance. God, he'd never seen eyes that colour before. Perhaps it was a trick of the light in this under-lit pub, but her blue eyes were an unusual shade, bright as cornflowers and emphasized by a fringe of coal-black lashes.

Her appraising gaze flicked over him. "I am."

"But you're a girl."

She glared, back stiffening.

"Okay, not a girl," he amended. "A woman." Very much a woman, all soft curves beneath the jeans and heavy work boots. She wore her ash-blonde hair up in a no-nonsense ponytail, probably more for convenience than style, and no make-up, not even a dash of lip gloss. Her only concession to her sex was the white collared shirt tailored just right for the swell of her breasts.

"Of course I'm a woman." She frowned. "What else would I be?"

He was saved from having to answer by the intrusion of a

stick-thin dyed blonde vacuum-packed in a cherry red dress who attempted to insert herself between them.

"Hi," the blonde breathed. "You're Ryan Morgan. I'm Cindy."

Of course you are. Cindy, Candy, Brandy. Their names were usually as indistinguishable as their faces. "Nice to meet you, Cindy. Do you mind? I'm in the middle of a conversation?"

"Oh don't mind me. I'm just leaving." Sam reached for the four pint glasses the barman set before her, balancing them in her small hands with practiced ease, and slipped away from the bar.

"What'll you have?" the barman asked.

"One of those." He nodded after the departing Sam, and willed the barman to hurry up so he could chase after her.

"I watch your TV show every week." The blonde. Was she still here?

"I sing too." She pouted a little, realising he hadn't yet bestowed his full attention on her, but still persistent.

"And I'm on vacation." He dropped his money on the counter, grabbed hold of his pint, and pushed past the blonde, heading for the tables on the lawn outside and the siren call of the first woman in years who *hadn't* thrown herself at him.

Sam was already seated with Nick and his mates when Ryan joined them.

"This is Ryan," Nick said, then to Ryan, "this is my crew." Nick swept an arm around the table, and performed the introductions; Drew, the local lord of the manor; Isaac, the brooding farrier recently returned from far-off places; novelist Daniel; Ken, the crew's newest recruit, and the twins, Ben and Jake, identical down to their matching dimples. The only way he could tell them apart was by the dreamy, *I just got laid* look in Jake's eyes. Lucky for Ryan he had a good memory for names and faces, or he'd be lost.

He sat astride the end of the bench beside Sam, and she shifted up to make space for him. Or more accurately, to make space between them.

"You're a firefighter too?" he asked.

She crossed her arms over her chest and raised her chin. "I am. You have a problem with that?"

He grinned. "You're certainly the prettiest fireman I've ever seen."

"Retained firefighter," she corrected. With a roll of her eyes, she turned away from him, swigging down a mouthful of beer. The brush off only intrigued him more.

"You're the hot shot talent scout on that TV show," said one of the twins.

That TV show, the reality talent show that had made him a household name. Ryan resisted the urge to roll his eyes as Sam had done. "That's me."

"You must get lots of chicks throwing themselves at you."

"All the time." Ryan suppressed a sigh, thinking of the dyed blonde in the pub whose name he'd already forgotten. "Trust me, it really wears thin after a while."

"Yeah right." Nick slapped him on the back. "Like that ever gets old."

"You're the one getting hitched. You tell me."

The entire table erupted with laughter as Nick blushed. "Lizzie's worth giving all that up for."

"You're a lucky man." And Ryan meant it. He wished he was in his friend's shoes, settling down with the one woman worth giving up all others for. He cast a sideways glance at Sam, and for a second their gazes met before she looked away.

The dyed blonde and her two friends had moved to an empty table nearby. They simpered and laughed just a little too loudly in the obvious hope of catching his attention.

"Oh well, guess that means the rest of us won't get a shot at any of the bridesmaids then, with you around," Isaac joked. Over his shoulder, the dyed blonde began to sing.

Sam coughed, covering a laugh.

"You're welcome to the bridesmaids." Ryan caught Sam's eye and grinned. "Especially if they think they can sing."

She smiled. An honest-to-goodness smile that lit up her eyes, which were no less stunning in colour out here in the sunlight.

"In fact, if Lizzie has any shy spinster girlfriends with absolutely no aspirations for their ten seconds of fame, I'll gladly volunteer to escort them to the wedding. The last thing I need is to spend an entire evening fending off desperate women with too much alcohol in them." That was the way he spent every other night of his life. He was tired beyond belief of the endless events he attended. More and more all he wanted was a real conversation over dinner. A real flirtation with some real chemistry.

"You can always take Sam. She doesn't have a date."

Yeah. That kind of chemistry.

Sam choked on the dregs of her beer. "That's exactly the way I'd like to keep it, thank you very much."

"Oh come on, Sam. It's not like bringing a date to the wedding would kill you," Nick said.

Sam glared at him. "You never know. It might. I'm ready for the next round. Whose shout is it?"

"I'll take this one." Ryan stood.

Nick also rose. "I'll help you with the drinks."

Back inside, Nick leaned against the bar as they waited for their order. "This is probably pretty tame compared to the fancy parties you usually attend."

"I'm enjoying this more than any party I've been to in years."

Nick studied him. "You know, that's not a bad idea I had."

"What idea?"

"If you're serious about wanting to avoid all the ambitious single women, you should bring Sam to the wedding. You'll be safe as houses with her."

"But will she be safe with me?" Ryan waggled his eyebrows and Nick laughed.

"You don't stand a snowball's chance in hell, mate. I've known Sam since we were kids, and you're not her type."

"What's her type?"

Nick wrinkled his nose. "Actually, I guess I don't know. It's never come up. Sam's just one of the guys. She's not that interested in men."

Or maybe just not in the men she'd known all her life and grown up with. But there'd been that look back at the bar, and her smile. Ryan had absolutely no doubt the right man would interest her. This weekend was really looking up.

"I'm game. Safe is my middle name."

Nick threw his head back in laughter. "Who are you, and what have you done with my friend?"

Chapter Two

"Are you crazy? Hell no!" Sam slammed the compartment door closed on the gear she'd meticulously stowed away in the fire truck.

"Please. It'd really help Ryan out. And it'll be much better than sitting at the loser table."

She stared at Nick as if she'd never seen him before. They'd known each other most of their lives, they'd done their training together. They'd even fought real flames together. And yet it was as if he still didn't know her at all. She set her hands on her hips. "So I'm just the sad, lonely loser who should be grateful for a date?"

"That's not what I said."

"It's what you think."

Nick squirmed and wouldn't look her in the eye. "Since you don't date, you'd be perfect for Ryan."

She frowned. "Who says I don't date?"

"Not once in all the time we've worked together have you hooked up with a guy. You're just not very...*girlie*...that way."

Just great. Was that how the rest of the crew saw her? Was that how the whole village saw her? Not that she hadn't found a man she wanted to date, but that she wasn't feminine enough to interest one? Well, she could do girlie if she wanted to. She'd show them all just how girlie she could be. Starting with that famous city slicker who oozed assurance like an expensive cologne.

"Fine. Tell your friend he can pick me up at three tomorrow. And if he isn't there on time I'll go to the church without him and he'll have to take his chances with the real girls."

"Oh come now, Sam, don't be like that. There's no need to be so sensitive."

She turned on her heel and stomped out the station. Ryan could finish packing away the gear on his own. She had a sculpture back in her studio that needed finishing and right now she wanted the company of twisted metal way more than she wanted the complications of people.

Chapter Three

The modern bungalow behind the fire station had no bell. Ryan rapped the door knocker twice and waited. He'd never seen a knocker quite like this before, a jagged lightning bolt made of metal. A feminine voice echoed inside, not distinct enough to make out words but he was pretty sure she said "come in."

He turned the handle and the door opened. *Who left their front door unlocked in this day and age?*

He pushed the door open and stepped into the hall. It was a standard entrance hall, narrow, with stairs leading upwards and an arched doorway to the right into a neat living room. Nice wooden floors, not too cramped. Spartan but comfortable.

"I'm through here."

He followed the sound of her voice down the passage into the kitchen at the back of the house. Attached to the side of the kitchen was a massive conservatory out of all proportion to the house, flooded now with afternoon sunlight.

Unlike the almost excessive neatness of the rest of the house, the conservatory was a cluttered mess, resembling the workshop of a mad inventor. Engine parts and broken appliances littered the work-benches, lying amongst tools he had no hope of recognising. The tang of singed metal filled the air.

In the centre of the room, Sam stood with her back to him, and for a heart-stopping moment he wondered if she'd decided not to go to Nick's wedding after all.

Then she turned. She wore work boots and a long white lab

coat spattered with grease and heaven only knew what, but she'd taken time to do her hair in an elegant chignon, and through her welding glasses he saw she wore make-up.

She removed the glasses. "You're early."

Her kohl-rimmed eyes seemed even bluer and more piercing than he remembered. "Nick read me the riot act. He said you're very hung up on punctuality."

Her full pink-painted lips curved into a smile. "He sent you early to make sure I didn't get carried away working and forget about the wedding. As if."

"What are you working on?"

She stepped aside to reveal a sculpture half a metre high of a couple locked in embrace. His temperature spiked. Against the backdrop of the cluttered workshop, and Sam's clinical attire, the eroticism of the sculpture came as something of a shock. Sam certainly had hidden depths.

She shifted her weight, drawing his attention back to her. "Can I get you something to drink? Tea, coffee..." She glanced at the wall clock, another metal creation, in the shape of a fire-spitting dragon. "Or something stronger?"

"Water will be fine." He licked his lips, his mouth suddenly dry.

She shrugged out of her lab coat, and his mouth got even drier. Beneath the coat she wore a hot pink cocktail dress, a simple above-the-knee design with scooped neckline and short sleeves. She looked as if she'd been poured into it. And her legs went on for miles. He swallowed. How the hell did Nick and his mates think this woman was 'just one of the guys'?

And just how many rhetorical questions was he going to ask himself tonight?

"Interesting shoes," he commented when she returned with a glass of water.

She glanced down and blushed. "I better change those before we go."

"No hurry. As you said, it's still early." He gave in to the insane urge to keep her talking. He wanted to get to know her, to peel away the defensive layers and uncover the woman within. Adrenalin surged through his veins, the same rush he got whenever an act stood on stage, ready to perform. Like the hushed moment in a theatre just before the curtain rose. That moment when anything might be possible.

He cleared his throat. "So, you're a sculptor?"

"Very clever, Sherlock. What gave me away?" Her cool gaze swept over him. "And you're a famous TV star."

"I'm just a talent scout who happened to get famous."

"Now that's an interesting career choice. Did you get out of bed one day and decide 'I'm going to get rich off of other people's talent'?"

He grinned. "What do you make your sculptures out of?"

"You're changing the subject."

"No, I'm not." He waved his arm around her studio. "You look at junk metal and see the potential for it to become something different, something more. I do the same with people. It's a rare gift we share."

Her eyes widened, as if surprised that he understood. Or perhaps surprised they had anything in common. "So what do you see in me?"

Not where he wanted to go. This was supposed to be a purely platonic date. Telling her she was the sexiest woman he'd laid eyes on in years wasn't platonic. "We should go if we want to get good seats in the church. And yes, now I'm changing the subject."

She pursed her lips to hide a smile and turned away. In the dining room she slid into a pair of heeled shoes in the same hot pink as her dress. Though the heels weren't nearly as high as the ones most women he knew wore, she wobbled in them as she stood.

She crossed to the mirror hanging over the fireplace to pin a fascinator to her sleekly coiffed hair. She struggled with a pin and he moved to stand behind her.

"Let me help you." He took the pin from her shaking fingers and carefully secured the simple arrangement of flowers in place.

Her gaze met his in the mirror, and this time they held. "Thank you." She didn't move. Her breathing seemed shallow.

He couldn't move either. The scent of her perfume, a delicate floral scent, enticingly feminine, wove around him, binding him. He was the one to look away first. *This was definitely not platonic.*

His gaze settled on the framed pictures on the mantel beneath the mirror. "Is that you?" The central photograph showed a man in full firefighter garb with his arms around a child of about eight or nine.

"Me and my dad just after we moved here."

"Where were you before that?"

"London."

"You don't miss it?"

"Miss what? I haven't been back there since." She broke eye contact and moved away.

His jaw dropped open. "You've never been back?"

She frowned. "It's not like I'm some country hick. It's just that everything I need is right here."

"A village full of men who don't even see you as a woman? Don't you want a relationship? Marriage, family and all that stuff?" The stuff every woman wanted. Hell, the stuff even he wanted.

She shook her head. "I'm much happier without all that. At least this way I don't have to wait for the axe to fall."

"What the hell are you talking about?"

"You know, that inevitable moment when the person you've invested all your happiness in ups and leaves."

His mouth quirked. "Are you always such a pessimist? Not everyone spends the entire relationship expecting it to end."

She shrugged into a lacy jacket and lifted her chin. "Well, they should. And I'm not a pessimist, I'm a realist. Now let's get moving before we really are late for this wedding."

Chapter Four

Sam hadn't been inside St Peter's Church since the day they buried her father. On the threshold, she sucked in a deep breath, and resisted the urge to grab Ryan's hand for support. Though why she suddenly felt a need for support, she had no idea.

There was only one person she could look to for strength and that was herself. Other people always let you down. They left, they died. She would face the memories just as she faced everything these days—alone.

"Are you okay?" Ryan's voice was low and surprisingly close.

She nodded. "Just fine." She squared her shoulders and prayed she could walk the length of the aisle without tripping in these ridiculous heels. This girlie thing was just stupid. Why did women put themselves through this?

The usher inside the door turned and smiled, his eyes heading straight to her exposed legs. His gaze travelled slowly up her calves, like a caress, and rather than the indignation she should have felt, a rush of power surged through her. *Oh, so that's why women suffered this torture.*

The usher's gaze carried on up, his smile curving a little deeper as he reached her chest. Then his gaze touched her face. He choked. "Sam?"

"Hi, Ken. You remember Ryan?"

Ken nodded mutely. He finally managed to close his mouth.

"We'll show ourselves to our seats, shall we?" She didn't wait for a response or to see if Ryan was still behind her. She headed down the aisle, face on fire as she concentrated on putting one foot in front of the other, and avoiding the glances burning in her direction. The conversation in the small church suddenly seemed muted.

Up at the front, Nick stood in conversation with the vicar and Daniel, his best man. As one, they turned at her approach. Nick whistled. "Look at you. You're a girl."

"Why is everyone so surprised by that? It's not like I had a sex change or anything."

The vicar's eyes rounded. Nick and Daniel both appeared dazed. And beside her Ryan laughed out loud. "I sincerely hope not!"

She blushed again. "What I meant is, congratulations." She shook Nick's hand. "I know you and Lizzie will be very happy together."

Seated in the pew, she finally let out the breath she hadn't realised she'd been holding. She'd done it. Not only had she not tripped, but she'd just proved to her entire crew that she could do the girlie thing. And she'd stood right in the spot where her father's bier had stood, without the slightest twinge.

A hand engulfed hers. She looked down, startled. A strong, masculine hand that sent a wave of warmth and support through her. She looked up into a pair of amused eyes the colour of molten metal.

Up close, he was even better looking than on TV. Dark hair cut short, a strong face with chiselled cheekbones and designer stubble. He grinned. "Now that wasn't so traumatic, was it?"

"How did you know?"

Ryan leaned close, his voice soft in her ear. "Because I know *you*."

God, she hoped not. She pulled her hand out of his grasp and crossed her arms over her chest, warding him off. Not that it helped. Awareness continued to ripple through her, like aftershocks from his touch.

The bridal march began and she rose, pasting on a smile.

She didn't need his understanding. She didn't need *him*. She didn't need anyone.

Chapter Five

Music thudded around them. With the meal cleared, speeches done, cake cut, there was nothing left to do but enjoy the party. Ryan leaned back in his chair and watched the bride and groom gyrating on the dance floor.

He turned to Sam. "Care to dance?"

"In these shoes? If I didn't put a heel through your foot, I'd probably trip and pull you to the floor."

"Now there's a thought, but we'll have to save that for later. In the meantime, take off your shoes and let's dance."

She had the prettiest blush, a slow, inexorable spread of heat up her cheeks. She didn't reply, perhaps couldn't, but she bent down and slipped off her shoes. He stood and held out a hand. The difference without the shoes was instantaneous. Sam relaxed, casting off the defiant slant to her shoulders. She smiled up at him. "I might still stand on your feet."

"You can try." He grinned. The mix of local draught, Cumbrian fresh air and her subtle perfume made him feel young and alive again. It made for a pleasant change from jaded and world-weary.

On the dance floor, he slipped an arm around her waist as they swayed to the music. Without the heels, she was grace in motion, fitting snugly against his body and sending a wave of heat through him that made the balmy summer evening outside the hall pale in comparison.

"Why fire fighting?" he murmured in her ear.

She lifted her chin. "Most people ask why metalwork."

"I'm not most people, and you haven't answered my question."

She smiled up at him, eyes burning bluer and brighter than the heart of a flame. "My father was a firefighter. It was his passion and he passed it on to me."

"The danger doesn't scare you?"

"There's very little danger. Only calculated risks, and we do our best to minimise even those." Enthusiasm lit her up. "Besides, fighting fires is the least of what we do."

"Tell me." He wanted to keep her talking, wanted to see that passion burn.

Instead, she pulled away. "I need a drink."

He frowned. Clearly Sam wasn't 'most people' either. Most people, when asked about their favourite subject, couldn't stop talking. He wondered, as he followed her to the densely packed bar, if she ever talked about herself. And if she ever let anyone really know her.

He muscled into the space beside her and leaned against the bar. "Where is your father now?" Certainly not here, he was sure. He didn't know why, but he was positive the girl in jeans and work boots had been Daddy's girl, and she wouldn't have worn a skirt this short with her old man around. This soft, curvy woman he'd held in his arms was a stranger not just to the people who knew her, but to herself as well.

"Six feet under."

"I'm sorry. Did he die on the job?"

She shook her head. "He would have liked that. No, he died of a heart attack."

#

Dad had often joked his broken heart would get him in the end. Sam swallowed pain that was still as fresh as it had been the day he died. As fresh as it had been the day Mum had packed a bag and said she'd be back soon. It had been two years before Dad accepted she wasn't ever coming back. And then within weeks he'd quit his job at the station, moved them north, and joined on as an RDS firefighter.

Sometimes she could still remember the way he'd been before mom left. He'd smiled more back then, and laughed more. Where other girls had grown up playing with Barbies, Dad had her rolling hose or building bonfires in the backyard, and they'd been happy.

Afterwards, he hadn't smiled so much, but it was still his smile she remembered better than anything else. He'd smiled as she'd climbed ladders faster than any of his other recruits, suited up faster, reacted quicker under pressure. She sometimes thought she had fire in her blood, and that's why it featured so much in her artwork.

"Earth to Sam."

She looked up into Ryan's cool grey eyes.

"What are you thinking about?"

She shrugged. "That there are things in life more frightening than fire." Now she really needed that drink. She waved for Tommy, the gangly student who also sometimes worked the weekend shift at the King's Head. "Scotch on the rocks."

"Make that two." Ryan leaned in beside her, his elbow brushing hers, a sharp reminder of this inconvenient chemical reaction she really didn't want to feel. "So you're not afraid of fire?"

She shook her head. "I'm not stupid; I have a healthy respect for fire. But no, I'm not afraid of it. Dad always said it's not fire that kills, it's carelessness."

Tommy set their drinks on the bar top.

"I'm guessing your father was a careful man." Ryan paid for the drinks and raised his glass. "And I'm guessing you're a careful woman."

She matched his toast. "I take care I don't get burned."

Chapter Six

They spent the next hour on the dance floor, moving together, touching, flirting, yet no matter how hard he tried to get her to open up again, Sam's shields were raised, impenetrable as any fire-wall. Her body might be willing, but her mind and heart were utterly closed.

But Ryan was not a man who gave up when he wanted something. The same instincts that made him a good talent scout also made him a killer agent. He never backed down when he was onto a good deal, and Sam was the best deal he'd found since… forever. He'd been hot for women before. He'd seduced his way into more hearts than he could count. But he'd never wanted someone like he wanted this cool, calm and collected woman who burned with fire inside.

The music turned soft and soulful, and Sam pulled away. He followed her off the dance floor. Many of the guests had already left. A few couples still clung to each other on the dance floor, including the bride and groom who seemed oblivious to the rest of the world. The bachelors, those firemen not on call tonight and who hadn't already left with the bridesmaids, grew increasingly rowdy around the bar.

"It's pumpkin hour." She wrapped the lacy jacket around her shoulders and faced him. A few strands of hair had worked loose from her chignon, brushing tantalisingly against the bare curve of her neck. Her cheeks were flushed, her eyes bright, but aside from that one drink she hadn't touched another drop.

"I'll walk you home."

"No need. This is probably the safest village in England."

He grinned. "I'm sure it is. I'm also sure you're quite capable of taking care of yourself."

She smiled at that.

"But I'm still walking you home."

A light breeze had arisen, and she shivered as the cool night air hit them. Ryan handed her his jacket.

"Thank you."

They walked down Church Lane in silence, and when they reached the low wall surrounding the graveyard, Ryan paused. Beyond the silhouette of the church lay the woods, dark and foreboding. It was perhaps the darkest place he could ever remember being. And with the sky clear tonight, it was also the most magical place he could ever remember being.

"Look up," he instructed.

Sam looked up, frowning. "What am I supposed to be looking at?"

"The stars. Each and every one of them is a ball of fire. Some burn hotter and brighter than others. Some are still new, and others are already dead and we just don't know it." A movement caught his eye and they both held their breaths as a shooting star flared and burned a trail across the velvet sky. "None of them are going to last forever, but can you imagine a world with no stars at all?"

He could only pray she knew he was talking about way more than basic astronomy.

A curtain twitched in an upstairs window of the nearest cottage. Sam turned away. "That'll be Mrs Cromaty. She's a daft old biddy, but if we hang around here much longer there'll be some very interesting gossip going round the village tomorrow."

"Would that be so bad?"

She shrugged. "You won't be here tomorrow. I will."

He grinned. "I think the bridesmaids will have provided

enough gossip to keep the rumour mill busy for a few weeks. Your reputation should be safe."

They turned into Back Lane. The fire station was almost in sight. Ryan took her hand, and felt rather than heard her breath hitch. He smiled, enjoying the connection between them, the promise of so much more.

#

They reached her front door too soon for Sam's liking. After an evening of delicious sexual tension, her body hummed with newly awoken needs, and she didn't want him to go. She wasn't ready for the night to end yet.

She hovered on the doorstep, fumbling with her latch key. "Would you like to come in for a cup of coffee?"

"I would love to, but I won't."

The rejection burned swift and deep. Had he been playing with her, the sad loser who couldn't get a date? Had the evening been nothing more than a joke to him? Tears stung the back of her eyes and she blinked them away. It certainly hadn't been a game for her.

Ryan took her free hand in both of his. "You're right. I won't be here tomorrow. And I suspect that's why you're inviting me in. You think I'm going to be a no-risk one night stand and you'll never have to see me again."

How did he do that? How did he know what she was feeling when even she herself wasn't ready to admit it?

"That's not enough for me."

Her gaze flashed to meet his. His cool gaze burned, setting her alight inside. Not a game at all. But then, why did it have to end? She swallowed against the sudden wave of fear rolling through her.

"I want to be worth the risk for you, Sam. I want you to stop hiding here in Coombethwaite and I want you to come to London and take a chance on this working out for us."

She shook her head slowly. "I can't do that, Ryan."

He leaned in close and pressed his lips to hers. It began as a mere brush of lips, a gentle taste, but like a spark on dry tinder, the flame fanned and the kiss became fierce and wild. He cupped her head, deepening the kiss, and her limbs turned molten. She clung to him for support.

When they broke apart, both breathless and wild-eyed, she took a step back into the solid, unyielding front door. She shook her head again. One kiss wasn't going to change anything, even if it was earth shattering. He asked too much of her.

His smile, so calm, so confident, pierced her. "You're braver than you think, Sam. I'll be waiting for you."

Chapter Seven

Ryan's offices were housed in a bright, shiny new building in Canary Wharf, surrounded by trendy coffee shops and scurrying, smartly dressed people. Sam rode the ten floors up, ignoring the lift mirrors and forcing her breathing to stay even. The doors slid open onto a large reception area, grey-carpeted with red and black furnishings.

The secretary barring the door to the inner sanctum was everything she'd expect for a man like Ryan. With a striking figure, and looking as if she'd just stepped from the pages of Elle, the woman looked over her designer steel-rimmed glasses at Sam as if she smelled bad and looked worse. And she'd even made an effort today. She'd left the work boots at home.

"May I help you?" The clipped accent was too perfect to be natural. Like her teeth and hair.

"My name is Samantha Redfern and I'd like to see Ryan Morgan."

"You and everyone else, honey. You don't have an appointment?"

"No I don't." She should have called. Perhaps she should have checked into her hotel, had a shower and changed first. Or perhaps she shouldn't have come at all. "Will you just give him something from me?"

"No CDs, no DVDs, no bribes." The secretary sounded so bored, Sam could only assume this happened every day.

She managed a smile. "No singing, I promise." She handed

over the small, neat package, wrapped in layers of plain white tissue paper.

The secretary barely gave it a glance before she set it on the edge of her desk. "You want to leave a business card with it?" she asked begrudgingly.

"He'll know who I am when he sees it." Assuming he didn't go around picking up metal sculptors every day. Assuming he didn't use the same lines he'd used on her on countless other women. Her heart pulled tight in her chest. This had been a mistake. She didn't really want to know.

If she'd never taken the risk, if she'd stayed safely at home in Coombethwaite, she'd never have to find out. Her heart wouldn't now be pounding, her palms wouldn't now be sweaty, and she would never have to face the possibility that he hadn't meant what he said and that he'd already forgotten her in the glitz and glamour of the big city.

But if she'd stayed home, she'd only have proved him right. She would have known that at heart she was a coward, too afraid to take anything but the most calculated risks. Like her father in more ways than one.

Sam took a deep breath and lifted her chin. "Please tell Ryan I'm staying at the Marriott until tomorrow morning."

She shouldered her overnight bag and turned to leave just as the door to the inner sanctum swung open.

"Sam?"

Her breath faltered.

He wore jeans and a shirt, just as he had the first day they'd met. This shirt was dark grey, gun metal grey, the colour of his eyes. She swallowed, and her breathing kick-started again. "Hi, Ryan."

"She brought you something," the secretary interjected, as if reminding them of her presence.

Ryan didn't even look in his secretary's direction. "What did you bring me?"

Me. If you'll have me. Sam nodded at the white package on the desk. Ryan crossed the room in a few easy strides and unwrapped the layers of tissue paper. He lifted the disk from the packaging and held it up.

"What is it?" The secretary no longer sounded bored.

"It's a shooting star." Ryan's eyes met Sam's.

"It's very rare. It's made from a real shooting star. Well, from a piece of meteorite."

Ryan smiled, and a slow burn ignited in the pit of her stomach. "Marilyn, please clear my diary for the rest of the day."

The secretary opened her mouth to protest, then closed it again. "Yes, Mr Morgan."

Sam's smile widened. Clearly *that* didn't happen every day.

Ryan held out a hand, and she took it, lacing her fingers through his. He gave a gentle tug and led her into his office, closing the door behind them. She got a brief impression of wide skyline and grey sky before he wrapped his arms around her, hands sliding down to hook in the back pockets of her jeans as he pulled her closer.

"So you made it all the way to the Big Smoke."

"I nearly turned back at least three times."

"You should have had more faith in yourself. I knew you could do it." His smile couldn't get any bigger. "You just needed to trust the fire inside."

About the author:

Romy Sommer lives in sunny South Africa where she works in the not-as-glamorous-as-you-think world of television advertising. When she isn't working or being mom to two young daughters, she can be found with her nose in a book. She writes flirty contemporaries, as well as more sensual historical novellas under the name Rae Summers.

Books by Romy
Waking Up In Vegas

Books by Rae
Prohibited Passion
Let's Misbehave
Dear Julia
An Innocent Abroad

A Smouldering Attraction

Suzanna Ross

Chapter One

Shelley Fox yawned as she unlocked her front door. It had been a tough night and she was tired through to her bones. Even her hair was weary. She couldn't wait to get into the shower and then into her comfy bed.

But first, a lovely cup of tea. She'd earned it. There had been four admissions onto her ward last night. Four children whose worried parents had, quite understandably, demanded answers from a reduced and overworked staff.

Food poisoning originating at the local nursery school had been suspected, but it would be a while before tests could confirm or deny that.

As she turned on the tap and filled the kettle, she naturally looked through the window and her gaze wandered over the picture-perfect cottage garden. It all looked especially splendid in the warm, morning sunshine. Seemed like it was going to be another hot day. When she'd had a couple of hours' sleep, she planned to sit outside with a book.

She hadn't thought so at the time, but she'd been lucky to have a reason to move out to Coombethwaite. And, even if it was a good distance from the hospital, she was happy she'd found this place.

Although it did need a lot of work on the inside. Number one on her list was decorating her bedroom—which she planned to do during the week off she had booked for later in the month.

After that, she'd look into extending the tiny kitchen, as some of her neighbours had done in their own cottages.

Distracted by something out of the corner of her eye, she looked towards her next door neighbour's garden. Something wasn't right. There were large clouds of smoke billowing over the hedge.

Odd. Her neighbour had entertained a niece and nephew-in-law to a barbecue yesterday—but this was more than dying charcoal embers.

"Oww." She jumped back from the sink as the kettle overflowed and cold water splashed over her top. She quickly turned the tap off, put the kettle down on the draining board and opened the back door.

"Hello?" she called. "Emily—are you there? Is everything okay?"

"Shelley, dear, the most awful thing's happened..."

Shelley had never heard her neighbour so upset. As a retired primary school teacher, Emily Croft had always been the epitome of calm and serenity.

"Hang on; I'm going to squeeze through the hedge."

Emily and the previous occupants of Shelley's cottage had been close friends and a narrow gap had been cut in the hedge so they could visit each other. The gap was overgrown now, but still thinner than the rest of the barrier—although it didn't seem like it as Shelley forced herself through the twigs and leaves. It was a relief to come out the other side. But that feeling was short-lived.

"What on earth?"

"It's the compost bin, dear. I went to put in the cold ashes from yesterday's barbecue and whoosh, this is the result."

"Oh dear. Have you phoned the fire brigade?" Shelley asked as she went for the hose pipe. Not that the puny jet of water made much difference, but it might stop the flames from taking hold of the rest of the garden.

"I should have put that in the shed. There's a hosepipe ban,"

Mrs Croft pointed out.

"So there is. But I think this is classed as an emergency. Please, phone 999."

"Yes, of course, dear. I'll go and do it now." She turned towards the house.

With a sigh, Shelley thrust the hose at her. "Keep it pointed towards the fire," she said as she fished her mobile from her pocket.

They were still trying to fight off the flames when the team of retained firemen arrived. If circumstances had been different, Shelley might have enjoyed the sight of Coombethwaite's finest parading through the garden in uniform.

But men, in uniform or otherwise, were the last thing on her mind these days. Besides, Mrs Croft was visibly distressed now and the fire was raging as fiercely as ever. She could feel the heat on her face and the flames were lapping at the cherry tree that stood far too near the compost bin.

There was shouting, there was action. These guys knew what they were doing. And, very soon, all there was to show for the drama was a charred corner of the garden and a teary Emily Croft.

Shelley gave her a quick hug and handed her a clean tissue from her pocket. "All over."

"I just feel so silly."

"It was an accident," one of the burly figures spoke. "It happens more often than you'd think."

"I'm sorry to have been such a nuisance."

He smiled reassuringly. "You weren't a nuisance. You did the right thing calling us."

Emily dabbed at her eyes with the tissue. "You're a good boy, Harrison."

Despite being so tired she could have fallen asleep on the spot, Shelley smiled. She guessed Harrison was an ex-pupil—this wasn't the first time she'd heard Emily speaking to former pupils as though they were still five years old.

But it never seemed so funny before—this man was in full fire fighting regalia and stood at least six-four.

She turned amused eyes towards him—and, despite everything, her heart soared when he caught her gaze and smiled.

"I try," he said, still smiling at Shelley.

And, with her eyes firmly fixed on Harrison's, Shelley felt rather than saw Emily Croft's interested look.

Chapter Two

Harrison had sworn off women. It was a long story and one he didn't like to visit often—but when you'd been walked over, humiliated even, in front of all your friends, family and work colleagues, it didn't do to risk a repetition.

As he looked at Shelley now, though, the thought occurred that maybe some things were worth the risk.

She really was extraordinarily pretty—even with her dark hair falling untidily out its severe bun and dark circles around her green eyes. Even the smudge of soot on her nose added to the overall picture.

"I don't know how it happened," Mrs Croft was telling him now. "The barbecue was stone cold—I promise it was. I even put my hand on it to check. And now I've disturbed everyone—called the fire engine out and not to mention bothering Shelley. And Shelley, dear, you must be exhausted. You're on night shift, aren't you?"

"Don't worry about that." Shelley smiled kindly. "Thank goodness I was here. I wouldn't like to think of you dealing with this on your own." She turned large green eyes towards Harrison. "If the barbecue was cold, what do you think might have happened?"

He pulled his gloves off and shoved them into a pocket of his coat. "When materials compost they can reach very high temperatures, they've even been known to combust spontaneously when there's been a prolonged dry spell like we've had recently."

"So maybe it wasn't anything Emily did?" There was a hopeful look in her eye. He liked that. Even without Emily Croft's confirmation of the fact, it was pretty obvious from the weary look on her face that she was freshly arrived from night shift. Yet she still cared enough to try to comfort her obviously distressed elderly neighbour.

He smiled, but he couldn't lie to her—in all probability there might have been a spark of something in amongst the ash. But he also didn't want to cause Emily Croft any more upset than she'd already suffered. "Maybe not. But it might be an idea not to empty the barbecue out onto the compost in future, just in case."

Emily nodded. "I'll make sure I don't. Thank you so much, Harrison—and thank Nick and Ben and the others for me, too."

Shelley patted her neighbour's arm. "Why don't you come over to mine for a bit? You've had a nasty shock and I was about to put the kettle on when I noticed the smoke. But we'll need to squeeze through the hedge—the front door's locked and I didn't bring my key."

Emily nodded. "Thank you, I'd like that. But just for a minute or two. You need your rest."

He watched in disbelief as the two women headed for the hedge. "Where are you going?"

"This is the way I came in," Shelley called over her shoulder. "Goodbye. And thanks." And then she pushed her way through.

He realised then the reason her hair looked like she'd been dragged through a hedge was because she had been.

#

Harrison found he couldn't focus. He had a set of drawings to finish for a client. His concentration would normally have been absolute. But, today, all he could think of was a pair of large green eyes.

He lasted a couple of hours before grabbing the keys to his

Land Rover and heading out the door.

He lived on the edge of Coombethwaite—only two minutes from the fire station in a home he'd designed for himself. A home that, on the side that looked out over the lake, was entirely glass and allowed the breathtaking scenery to be a part of his everyday life.

Really, he should be walking the short distance, but he was on duty and if his pager went off, he wouldn't be allowed the luxury of a leisurely walk—or even a run. He'd need the Land Rover.

He reached the row of cottages where only hours ago he'd pulled up in a large red truck. And hesitated for only a minute before knocking.

Mrs Croft opened the door within minutes and smiled when she saw him. "Harrison, what a lovely surprise."

"I wanted to make sure you were okay," he told her. "You seemed pretty shaken up this morning."

"I'm fine." She smiled bravely. "Why don't you come in? It would be nice to have a chat and catch up on all your gossip."

He followed her into the kitchen and accepted the cool homemade lemonade she offered. "Thanks." The afternoon was warm and the drink pleasantly cold.

"Shelley looked after me so well this morning," she said as she sat beside him at the table with her own drink. "Such a nice girl, you know."

"I gathered."

"She's single." Emily Croft raised an eyebrow.

Although it was an answer to a question he'd been burning to ask, it wouldn't do to show interest. "And what's her marital status to do with me?"

"One of these days, Harrison Reid, you'll let go of that giant chip on your shoulder and realise what's good for you."

"I hope you're not trying to set me up with your neighbour. Because you know what happened the last time someone introduced me to a woman who was supposed to be perfect for me."

He tried not to wince. His fellow fire fighters had thought they were doing him a favour. How were they supposed to know the mystery siren newly arrived in the village would declare undying love for him the same day she accepted a proposal of marriage from her city boyfriend?

Mrs Croft laughed softly. "Harrison, how could you think such a thing? Setting you up with Shelley was the last thing on my mind."

Harrison didn't believe her for an instant, but he grinned anyway. "Good."

"But Shelley was telling me this morning that she's thinking of extending her kitchen. I told her I knew a good architect..."

Harrison's grin turned into a laugh.

"She's sitting in her garden—I saw her when I was shaking my duster from the upstairs window right before you arrived. Why don't you go and have a word? It will be a nice little job for you."

Chapter Three

It was a hot day and getting hotter. Shelley shifted sleepily on her sun lounger—even though she was in the shade and covered head to toe in factor 50, she knew the sensible thing to do would be to go inside until later.

Her book was slipping from her fingers, her eyes closing, she knew she should move, but she was so comfy out here in the sun and she'd had very little sleep...

"Hey," a man's deep voice reverberated around her garden and, startled, she sat up and pushed her sunglasses into her hair.

A head poked through the thin spot in the hedge. A dark-haired head with grey eyes and the sort of perfect bone structure that made her want to weep.

"Harrison?" She wasn't sure—she'd only seen him once after all and a fireman's uniform disguised a lot. As did a nurse's scrubs. Her face flushed as she realised just how exposed she was here in the garden wearing only a tiny black bikini.

He pushed his large frame through the hedge and stood looming over her. Disturbingly, his black tee-shirt left his arms bare and his denim jeans drew far too much attention to his powerful thighs. She looked away, resisting the urge to run and hide.

"Hello." His teeth flashed white in his tanned face and his laser-sharp eyes searched her face with undisguised interest. "Am I disturbing you?"

"Not really, I'm only enjoying the sunshine—need the vitamin

D." She smiled to cover her embarrassment, knowing she was babbling.

"I was here to make sure Mrs Croft was okay—after earlier."

She nodded.

"She's a friend of my gran's, as well as my old primary school teacher. I've known her all my life."

"Which explains why she talks to you like you're a five-year-old?"

He laughed. "Exactly."

Shelley's smile faded. "Is she okay? She still seemed a bit shaken when she left. But she insisted on going—said she didn't want to be a bother."

"She seems fine. She's tougher than she looks."

He sat on the edge of her sun lounger and she took in a deep breath. He was too close and the garden that had seemed big enough was suddenly too small.

"She said you're thinking of extending your kitchen."

Nothing was secret in Coombethwaite, Shelley was quickly learning that truth. "She was singing your praises as an architect as soon as I mentioned it. I suppose she's sent you to get the job?"

He laughed. "She did suggest I might want to speak to you about it."

"I'm sorry to disappoint, I don't think I could afford someone with your talents."

He raised an eyebrow.

"It's not only me she talks about. She's very proud of your achievements."

He rubbed his chin. "What if I don't charge you?"

"Sorry?"

"What if, in exchange for helping you with your kitchen extension, there was something you could do for me in return?"

Shelley immediately drew her knees up to her chest and hugged them tight. "I don't know what you think I am, but…"

He looked as horrified as she felt and two hot spots of red appeared on his razor sharp cheekbones. "No." He lifted a large hand in the international 'stop' gesture. "No. Nothing like that."

Shelley's face still burned. She was so mortified, she could barely bring herself to meet his gaze. "What then?"

"I need a date for my friend's wedding next week."

Shelley's face burned. "I'm not looking for a relationship."

"Neither am I. All I'm looking for is a platonic companion so my friends will stop trying to set me up."

#

Shelley didn't quite know how he'd talked her into it—well, she did, and it had nothing to do with any architect's drawings. First, he was gorgeous and any woman would enjoy attending an event with him on her arm.

He's a trophy fireman. She giggled at the thought.

Secondly, he'd made it clear he was as disinterested in any romantic shenanigans as she was.

He'd promised Shelley a night of uncomplicated fun where she could meet more of her new neighbours. And, still being so new in the village, she wasn't in any position to turn him down.

She was ready when he arrived to pick her up.

"You look lovely," he said.

"You don't need to say that. It's not really a date, is it?"

"No. But you do look nice, and I wanted to tell you."

She smiled. He looked pretty hot himself, but she decided not to mention it in case it turned into an impromptu and embarrassing meeting of the mutual appreciation society.

She'd always loved weddings and this one was just perfect. The church was crowded. Nick, the groom, was handsome and Lizzie, his bride, gorgeous. It was, in fact, everything a summer wedding should be.

"Would you like to dance?" he asked as couples took to the floor at the reception.

"Yes, thank you."

It was odd how comfortable she was in Harrison's arms. He gathered her close and she rested her head on his shoulder.

As the music finished, he took her hand and led her outside. "Hot in there," he said. "We should get some air."

They walked a little way around the lake. The evening light was stunning and the scenery had never looked better. If Shelley had ever been of a mind to let romance muddle her brain, this was the kind of night it might happen.

Thankfully, she was immune to that sort of stupidity.

"Do you want to tell me about it?"

She blinked. "Tell you about what?"

They'd stopped short of the pebbled waterline. She'd have liked to go closer, but reckoned she shouldn't risk it in her heels.

"About why you're so adamantly against getting involved with someone?"

She looked out across the water and tried to concentrate on the beauty of the scenery. But it was impossible when the man at her side commanded her attention. "It's not something I want to talk about."

He was silent for a moment, but she could feel his gaze on her. Her heart thudded in her chest. Everyone had been nagging her for ages to get on with her life—meet someone else, have a fling.

And the prospect had never been more tempting.

He took a step closer.

Relocating to this gorgeous village had been the first move in her recovery. Having fun with this man might be the next one...

He reached out and lifted her chin so she looked into darkened grey eyes.

Her heart nearly stopped beating.

"Who was he? Is he worth denying yourself the chance of future happiness?"

When Harrison's lips met hers in the briefest of butterfly kisses, she was quite sure it wasn't.

Chapter Four

Harrison couldn't leave it alone.

One night—and an entire morning— with Shelley in his arms was all it had taken for him to realise.

If he was prepared to put his nasty experience and very public humiliation behind him, then he had to try to show Shelley it could be done. That she could forget whatever—whoever—had hurt her.

"I thought she was the one, and I was gutted when I found out what she was like," he told her as he drove her home from his house the day after the wedding. "For a long time I didn't think it would be possible to fall for someone else."

"What made you change your mind?"

He brought the Land Rover to a stop in front of her cottage and turned off the engine. His gaze unwavering, he looked into her green eyes. "I met you."

"Oh, Harrison." She sighed. "I like you, of course I do. But the thought of trusting a man again…"

"Last night was good, wasn't it?"

"It was one night."

He leaned back into his seat. "What did he do to you?"

She laughed, but he could see it wasn't funny. "The usual—he couldn't keep it in his pants." The defiant look in her eyes dared him to argue.

He found he couldn't resist the challenge. "He was an idiot. But we're not all the same."

"I know." She smiled a little sadly. "But it's too much trouble to try to sort the good guys from the bad. I just want a quiet life."

He sighed. He knew what she was talking about—he'd been in that place a long time, trying to work out which women were liars and cheats. But now he was ready to love again and he didn't doubt for an instant that Shelley was someone he could trust with his heart.

"I'm sorry, Harrison. Maybe if I'd met you at a different time…"

He reached out and took her hand. "Don't say that," he pleaded. He didn't want platitudes—especially not the same ones he'd trotted out to every woman who'd set her cap at him in the past two years.

She let her hand rest in his and they sat for a moment. It was funny, for a man who'd spent the past few years being suspicious of attractive women, his intuition had told him straight away she was someone worth falling for. Perhaps it was the kindness she'd shown Emily Croft—despite her obvious weariness after a hard night's work.

And, the moment he'd gate-crashed her garden and seen her in that bikini, he'd been forced to admit his interest was very personal.

It killed him she didn't feel the same.

His only hope was she'd learn to trust him in her own time. "Okay, how about we see each other as friends?"

He watched as she bit even white teeth into the flesh of her lower lip. "Okay, Harrison Reid," she said at last. "I think I might like that."

Better than nothing, even if it wasn't the outcome he'd hoped for.

#

She went into her cottage without even glancing back. He waited until she'd closed her front door before he turned the key in the ignition. And that was when the summons to go into the station arrived.

"It's a big one," Jake told him with a shudder as he arrived and boarded the fire engine with the others. "The biscuit factory's gone up."

The factory was a family concern, employing around thirty local people. He only hoped everyone had been evacuated safely.

The flames were visible as soon as they arrived. "We're worried about the flour stores," the manager told them with a frown. "I've heard powders like that can explode."

"If there's enough flour suspended the air it's a possibility," Harrison told the woman. "Make sure everyone's well clear of the building. Do we know what happened?"

She shook her head. "It started in the office, I think. There wasn't anyone up there at the time. We told people to get out as soon as we noticed."

"And everyone's safe?"

She nodded. "I think so. The team leaders have checked and nobody's reported any absences."

"Tina," someone called. "Tina's not here."

Harrison quickly found out the missing worker's likely location and then, with Daniel, went into the factory to search.

He never thought of himself as being brave, but it took a huge dose of courage to walk into a burning building—every time.

The heat was intense, even through the protective layers of his clothing. And there was smoke everywhere, making visibility poor. He knew if it wasn't for their breathing apparatus, he and Daniel wouldn't have stood a chance.

Something crashed behind him. He turned to see debris flying through the air.

And that was the last thing he remembered.

#

Harrison grew aware of noise. Voices… muffled as though from long way away. And pain—he could feel pain. A dull ache in his head and every other part of him hurt, too.

"Harrison, can you hear me?" One of the voices was closer now, sharper. A woman's voice. She sounded like Shelley.

He tried to say her name, but his throat was parched and the words wouldn't come.

"Don't try to talk," she told him. "You're okay. You were in an accident. You got caught in falling masonry at the biscuit factory fire. But you're safe—in hospital. You're going to be fine."

He believed her.

He forced his eyes open. And there she was. Blurred at first, and then her face came into sharp focus.

Even in her scrubs and without a scrap of makeup, she was gorgeous.

Despite feeling like hell, he managed to grin.

And her lips curved in a response that had his heart beating faster.

Heck of a thing that a man had to nearly get himself killed to get her to smile at him like that.

Her smile was the last thing he saw as the medication took a hold of him again and he drifted off to sleep.

#

Next time he came to, there was no sign of Shelley, but a male nurse was in the room.

"Hello there," he greeted. "I'm Terry. Good to have you back with us."

"Tina?" Harrison managed to croak.

"Ah—our other casualty from the fire. She's going to be fine."

Harrison heaved a mental sigh of relief. They hadn't lost anyone in the time he'd been with the fire service, but there was always the fear it might happen. "What about my colleague, Daniel?" He spoke a little easier now. "He was in the fire with me."

"He's fine."

Having satisfied himself that those in danger were safe, he

couldn't help himself asking the next question. "And Shelley?" His voice was stronger still.

As he looked into the nurse's face, Harrison could have sworn he saw a bleak look cross the other man's features. But he must have imagined it because the next moment the man smiled. "She's on duty in paediatrics, but she'll be here soon. She popped in to see you first thing and said she'd be back when her shift was over."

Chapter Five

Shelley knew she shouldn't be lusting after a patient. Particularly when she'd already assured the same patient she had no romantic interest in him. And especially not when the patient in question was out of it and had no idea.

However gorgeous he might be, however tempting it was to look at him, that kind of behaviour was kind of gross and she hated herself for it.

Besides, after the scandal her last relationship had caused, she wanted to keep any hint of romance firmly out of the hospital.

She couldn't bring herself to leave, though.

When she'd heard Harrison was being brought in, she'd been shattered.

And her reaction had proved without doubt—and regardless of anything she'd told him—that she did care about him. A lot.

She even suspected it might be love.

In the startlingly short time she'd known him, he'd grown into the most important person in her life. She felt all kinds of fool that she'd only realised her feelings when she'd thought she might lose him.

His eyes fluttered open. And, when he saw her, he smiled.

"Hi." His voice was groggy, but less so than it had been yesterday.

She smiled back, grateful he sounded so much more like himself. "Hello. How are you feeling?"

"Like I've been run over by a truck and kicked in the head by a horse. But I'm told I'll live."

"Which is a huge relief to a lot of people."

"You included?"

She shook her head in disbelief. "How can you even ask me that?"

"Is that a yes?"

"Of course it's a yes," she leaned over and dropped the briefest of kisses on his forehead. She hovered over him, reluctant to sever the moment of closeness.

The door of Harrison's side room opened.

She jumped away as a nurse came into the room.

Terry's eyes narrowed as he took in the scene. "Here again, Shelley?"

He was adept at making her feel bad, but she wasn't going to let him get away with it this time. She was stronger now. Not the doormat she'd been when she'd wasted two years of her life dating him.

"Nothing wrong with your eyesight, is there, Terry?"

His expression borrowed more from a grimace than it did a smile, but he checked Harrison with all the professionalism she would have expected before leaving the room. He might have been a rotten boyfriend, but he was a good nurse.

"Was that him?"

She nodded.

"He's an idiot for letting you go."

She smiled.

"If you were mine I'd think myself the luckiest man in the world."

"Harrison, this is where I work. We can't have this conversation here."

"But you can kiss me on the forehead?"

He was right, of course, that had been unprofessional in the extreme. "A momentary lapse."

He was quiet for a moment. "I'm not so injured you can't

have another lapse and kiss me properly."

"Were you listening to what I said a moment ago?" she asked softly. "We can't do anything about our personal relationship. Not when you're a patient at the hospital where I work."

For someone who'd spent much of the past two days semi-conscious, he was remarkably quick on the uptake. His expression said it all and it took all her willpower to stop herself getting into bed beside him.

"What about when I'm no longer a patient at the hospital where you work?"

She experienced another momentary lapse—although not quite the one Harrison had suggested—and reached out to cover his hand with her own. "When you've been discharged, we can talk about what we both want."

#

By the time her shift finished the next day, Shelley was trembling with the need to see him. It couldn't lead to more—not yet at least. But just being in the same room as him was better than nothing.

To hear his voice. To know he was okay.

When she found his room empty, his bed stripped, she could barely breathe.

"Looking for lover boy?" Terry asked with a malicious tone.

She rounded on him, although she stopped herself grabbing his shoulders and shaking the truth from him. "Where is he? He's not..."

Terry sighed. "No, he's not. He's discharged himself. Against medical advice."

She ran out to the car park and cursed the distance between the hospital and Coombethwaite. After what seemed like a million years, she drew into the outskirts of the village and drove past her own cottage to get to Harrison's house.

She'd only been there once before—the evening of his friend Nick's wedding. She smiled as she recalled that night. Then she reminded herself to be cross again as she drove in through his gate.

He'd been so irresponsible. She was furious with him. And she'd waste no time in telling him when he answered the door.

Her resolve weakened when she saw him.

But the shock of seeing this big man so pale and clinging onto the door frame for support only silenced her for a moment.

"Look at you," she yelled. "What kind of idiot goes against a doctor's advice like this? You live on your own; you can't even answer the door without nearly collapsing in pain."

Infuriatingly, he stood there, saying nothing, but his grin had her tummy fluttering and her breath catching. Then, despite the support of the door jamb, he swayed unsteadily and she relented.

"Come on, let's get you inside." She helped him in, although she suspected her contribution was more mental than physical: Despite her arm being about his waist and his around her shoulders, he put very little of his weight on her.

"Why did you go against medical advice?" she asked when he was safely settled on the sofa. "You're in no fit state to care for yourself."

"Perhaps I'm not," he agreed. "But at least now I'm no longer in your hospital we can date."

She felt two angry spots of colour on her cheek and stormed over to loom over him. "Seriously? You put your life in danger just so I'd go out with you? I've never heard of anything so stupid."

Unfazed, he reached up and his big hand circled her wrist. When he tugged, she willingly fell onto the sofa to lie alongside him.

And found she could no longer be angry with him. Even if he deserved it.

"Isn't this nice?" he asked and she sighed.

"Yes, it is."

"Shelley, this is where you belong. And you know it."

"But…"

"Do you honestly think I could lie in that hospital a moment longer when you'd told me we could be together once I was discharged?"

"But I didn't mean for you to leave before a doctor agreed you were ready."

"I'm fine. I promise you. I wouldn't have left if I wasn't sure of that."

"I still don't like the thought of you being here alone."

"Then move in with me."

His breath was warm on her face and she couldn't think properly. But she knew what he said made sense. Apart from anything else, she wanted to look after him. "I've got annual leave booked for the next week. I was going to decorate my bedroom, but I suppose I could stay here and keep an eye on you instead."

"The next week will be a start."

She sighed and snuggled as close as she dared without risking hurting him. And then, tempted to the point of distraction, she kissed him full on the lips.

He tasted delicious—warm and uniquely right.

"I could get so used to this I might never want to let you go." He spoke against her mouth and she felt his words right through her body. They made her shiver. "I love you, Shelley."

"Maybe I don't want you to let go." And, to prove the point, she kissed him again. "Because I love you, too, Harrison," she finally admitted when she came up for air.

About the author

Suzanna Ross writes sweet, modern romances and a number of her short stories have been published in women's magazines in the UK and in Australia. She also writes as Suzanne Ross Jones. Suzanna and her family live in Scotland. With dramatic hills, mysterious lochs and romantic castles on her doorstep, she finds she can't help but be inspired.

By Suzanna Ross
Trust In Me
Hidden Heartache

By Suzanne Ross Jones
The Baby of the Family & Other Stories
Your Secret Smile (Montcraig Sweethearts)

Locked Into Love

Catherine Coles

Chapter One

Cassie pulled ineffectually at the handcuffs holding her wrist securely to the desk. No, it wasn't going to work. Little Ed had definitely fastened the pink fluffy handcuffs and taken the key with him. She pulled one last time, the noisy clank of metal on metal sounding overly loud in the quiet newsroom.

She'd been back in Coombethwaite for precisely two days and already she wished she'd stayed in London. Although, after being made redundant, she couldn't afford to keep up the payments on her Canary Wharf apartment. She didn't really have much choice but to return to the village she'd left eight years ago with plans of taking Fleet Street by storm and never returning to her childhood home.

Of course, as is the case in villages, everyone knew she was back with her tail between her legs and her dreams in tatters.

She'd thought begging her old boss, Harry Swales, for a job on the local newspaper was the pinnacle of her humiliation. That was until she heard the distinctive rumble of the fire truck outside. *No, no, no! This was not going to happen. Fate wouldn't be so cruel. Would it?*

Surely it wasn't possible to sink further into the pool of humiliation. How could it get worse than being attached to an old fashioned metal desk with your own handcuffs?

The fire engine came to a stop outside the newspaper office and through the open door she heard feet landing on the path outside.

"Hello?" A deep voice called from outside. Cassie's insides clenched and she pulled again at the restraint hoping against hope that a miracle had occurred and she could escape.

Heavy footsteps sounded on the wooden floor of the outer office and a head poked into the main room where Cassie sat on the worn carpet in a puddle of despair. She ducked her chin into her chest and let her hair fall over her face. Maybe if she …

"Cassie Parker. What mess have you got yourself into now?" His dimples winked at her as though he was replaying every one of her childish pranks in his head.

She threw back her shoulders and readied herself to give a haughty, plausible explanation for her situation. Unfortunately she forgot about the metal desk and her head banged back against one of the legs. Tears smarted in her eyes and her hatred for Little Ed overtook that for the man in front of her.

Ben Spencer. Her childhood sweetheart and the man the whole of Coombethwaite, including herself, had thought she was certain to marry.

Cassie's mortification multiplied as the rest of the crew crowded behind Ben trying to see what was happening.

"We need cutting equipment," Ben turned and spoke quietly. "Cassie needs cutting free."

Her cheeks burned as sounds of obvious amusement outside floated in on the summer air through the open office windows. A commotion sounded in the outer office before Little Ed stumbled in, a huge grin stretching his thin cheeks.

"Aha!" he crowed. "Fireman rescues damsel in distress!"

"No." Cassie shook her head.

Ben seemed to realise what Little Ed was going to do and crouched in front of Cassie a moment before the flash of Ed's camera lit up the room.

If not for Ben, her awful colleague would've recorded her mortification for the whole village's entertainment. Gratitude warred with annoyance and something else entirely. She hadn't been prepared for the effect seeing Ben again would have on her.

He'd always been tall and muscular due to the demanding physical nature of running a farm but now he filled his uniform so well her mouth went dry, her tongue sticking to the roof of her mouth. She hoped his impossibly broad back had shielded her from Ed's camera.

"Out!" Ben's voice boomed in the small room. She peered around him, gratified to see Little Ed's face crumple. Gone was the triumphant smile. Ben got to his feet and walked casually towards the other man. "It's time to leave."

Cassie choked back a giggle as Little Ed scurried off like the rat he was.

"So," Ben knelt next to her again. "Let me check your head and then you can tell me how on earth you've got yourself into this mess."

Cassie wanted to argue with him, tell him this wasn't one of her infamous scandals, but given her predicament she thought it best to remain quiet. She bent her head forward so Ben could check the spot where she'd hit the metal table leg.

As soon as he put his hands onto her sensitive scalp, any thoughts of speech she may have had disappeared and her ability to form even sensible thoughts ended. Cassie pursed her lips together to stop the sigh of pleasure from erupting.

Ben's chest was level with her eyes and his familiar scent washed over her. He smelled of outdoors, of hard work and something that was entirely Ben. Her stomach dipped as her thoughts turned to the fun they could have had with these handcuffs. Privately. With no clothes on.

This time she let the sigh out. That was never going to happen. He'd broken her heart once and she wasn't about to let him do that again.

"Okay." He took his hands from her head and tilted it back gently so he could look at her. "The skin is abraded but there's no free flowing blood. How do you feel?"

"Ridiculous, exposed ..."

"I meant your head. How does your head feel where you banged it?"

"Oh." Cassie's eyes locked onto his beautiful grey ones and she felt horribly near tears again. "It feels fine."

If he saw the emotion she was struggling to contain, he mercifully didn't say anything. Instead, he became all business-like as he strode to the outer office and asked for the cutting equipment.

Crouching back down beside her, he felt around her wrist. "These are on pretty tight. If you can hold one side tight against your wrist, I'll cut the other side where there's a slight gap. Is that okay?"

Cassie nodded, not trusting herself to speak. At least, not trusting that any words that came out of her mouth would answer the question he'd asked or make any sort of sense.

"How did this happen, Cass?"

"Little Ed." She spat out his name, using as much derision as she could.

"You know," Ben started as he snipped the metal holding her captive. "No one really calls him Little Ed anymore."

"Because he's not so little?" Ed Swales towered over her, he was at least six foot five and had grown a foot and a half since she last saw him.

"And he's not a kid any more. Some things changed when you left, Cassie."

She didn't like the censorious tone in his voice—as though she somehow were to blame for leaving Coombethwaite. The way she remembered it, he'd broken her heart and she'd rushed off to the train station and only stopped sobbing somewhere around the midlands.

As the handcuffs fell away from her wrist, she rubbed the reddened skin. "You haven't changed though, have you, Ben?"

He got to his feet, the broken handcuffs dangling uselessly

from the fingers of one large hand.

"No," he straightened powerful shoulders and stared down at her. "I haven't changed at all."

Cassie wasn't sure whether that was a good thing or not. It meant that everything she'd once loved about Ben remained the same but everything that had infuriated her—what she'd once seen as his complete lack of ambition—had remained exactly the same.

"I should go," he said, making no moves to leave the cramped newspaper office. His eyes shone with merriment. "But I really can't leave until I know how you came to be fastened to the desk with these."

Cassie got to her feet and made a grab for the handcuffs. Ben was much too fast for her and sitting in one place for so long had given her pins and needles in her feet that made even standing precarious let alone chasing Ben for her ruined handcuffs.

"Ed." She looked around for him as though he were still lingering. "He said he had a tip for a great story but only one of us could go. I bent under the desk to grab my bag and he had the handcuffs ready and fastened them."

"That's ..."

"Humiliating."

"Well, yes," he agreed. "But I was going to say it's pretty ingenious. For Ed."

There was no way Cassie was going to agree with him. It was hurtful, unnecessary, not to mention downright criminal.

"So," he held up the handcuffs. "I'm thinking these aren't Ed's?"

"Nope, they're mine." She met his gaze steadily.

A hint of colour spread across his tanned cheekbones. He took a step towards her. "What are you doing with pink fluffy handcuffs, Cass?"

He was now standing way too close and his low voice

skittered her senses, his lips nearly touching her ear. His nearness made it hard to think, to form a sentence. "They were for a story."

She kept her gaze on his chest, not daring to meet his eyes, knowing she was barely hanging onto her sanity as it was. If she looked at him she'd be lost.

"What kind of story would need handcuffs?"

"I did a story on parties. You know the sort, a saleswoman comes to your home and you can buy lingerie and ... um ... other stuff."

"Other stuff?"

Ben's eyebrows rose as though his question was genuine, but she knew better. She was also tired of his teasing. It was past time for her to regain her control.

"Yes." She trailed a hand down his chest, stopping at the top of his trousers. "You know exactly what I mean."

"Okay, well, I think I'd better be ..."

"Oh you don't want to leave, Ben." Cassie closed the space between them. If he wanted to tease, she'd show him she could tease a whole lot better than he could. "I got a great deal on some of the items on sale. I remember how much you liked the colour red."

"I ..."

"Close the door, Ben." Cassie undid the top button of her blouse. "I'll show you, shall I?"

He licked his lips, darting a look behind him, then back at Cassie. Running his hands down her back he cupped her bottom and pulled her towards him.

"Spencer! What you doing in there?"

Ben groaned. "On my way."

Cassie shrugged, feigning nonchalance even as her heart beat faster than the infuriating ticking of the old clock hanging on the office wall. "Some other time, maybe."

She didn't mean it. She was going to stay as far away from

Ben Spencer as she could but he didn't need to know that. Playing the sophisticated big city flirt was a front.

She was never going to let him know how much he'd hurt her and the only way to avoid it happening again was to quit the job she'd begged for and get the hell out of Coombethwaite.

Chapter Two

"So, you going to answer me?" Drew asked as Ben climbed back into the fire engine. "What were you doing in there all that time?"

"Can't a guy have a conversation with a lady he's just rescued?"

"Not when the lady in question is the reason you've never got past more than three dates with another woman since she left."

"That's not true. Last year Claire Cooper and I ..." Ben couldn't even finish his sentence. They were right. No one had ever come close to Cassie. No one had made him feel even a fraction of the love he'd had for her.

Hell, his hands still tingled from touching her, the feel of her bottom in his hands taunting him—he had to stay away from her. He'd finished their relationship and he'd had a damn good reason for it. There was no way he could let her get her hot little hands anywhere near him again.

He'd teased her and she'd given it back tenfold.

"Yeah ...you went out a couple of times until you realised her hair colour was from a bottle and no one had the same wheat coloured hair as Cassie."

Ben frowned. "I did *not* say that."

"Yeah," Isaac agreed. "You did."

"If I was drunk then comments like that do not count."

"You've got it wrong," Sam commented as she negotiated the fire truck through the country lanes. "When you're drunk your comments matter a whole lot more because they come from your subconscious. They are what you really feel."

"Rubbish."

That couldn't be right, could it? He surely wasn't sabotaging every relationship he began simply because the other girls weren't Cassie? He'd let her go. He'd done the right thing. She'd moved on, he'd moved on.

So why was it when he closed his eyes, all he could see was a field full of wheat, dancing in the summer sun and Cassie's smile mocking him?

Chapter Three

"Prove it!" Ben tried to ignore the childish dare.

"Yeah," Daniel agreed as he put his pint back down on the table in front of them. "Prove she means absolutely nothing to you."

Ben wished he'd given Nick and Lizzie's wedding a miss. He was sure he could've made up some disaster at the farm. It wasn't as though people would disbelieve his story. Everyone in the entire village knew he was in danger of losing his farm. It just wasn't economically viable any more, but Ben refused to give up.

"And how would I do that?" He wasn't going to take up his friends' dare. But it would be interesting to find out how they thought he could prove he was completely over Cassie.

"Dance with her." Marcus suggested.

"Dance? No way." Ben shook his head for extra emphasis. He was a farmer. A big man whose feet worked best in a pair of wellies trudging through fields looking after four legged animals. They did not belong on a dance floor.

He glanced over to where Cassie sat with her friends. Her scarlet dress skimmed over the rise of her breasts, the hem brushing the floor. Wispy blonde tendrils framed her cheeks. No, dancing with her was out of the question. He'd stand on her feet or trip over and make a fool of himself. Wasn't happening.

"Yeah, you know, you just stand with each other on the dance floor and wave your arms about a bit."

Ben downed what was left of his pint. "I don't think so."

Harrison shrugged. "Then I guess just being near her *will* cause you some problems?"

"Not at all," Ben denied even as his stomach clenched—simply thinking about having Cassie near him was a bad idea. He'd nearly combusted yesterday when she'd touched him.

"So you should do it. Prove your point." His twin Jake goaded.

"Will it stop you lot harassing me and mentioning her name every time you speak to me?"

The knowing smiles, nudges and winks that followed told Ben he'd fallen neatly into their trap. They'd baited him and he'd fallen for it. He couldn't lose face now otherwise they would never let up. Working as a volunteer fireman was something he felt passionately about and his colleagues were also his friends, but right now he could cheerfully never speak to any of them ever again.

"Right." Ben pushed to his feet and looked over at Cassie once more. "One dance. Easy."

He made his feet move while the part of his brain not controlled by macho bravado told him what an idiot he was. He was a farmer. A fireman. But definitely not a dancer.

"Hey Ben," Cassie's lips stretched into a smile but her voice betrayed her reluctance.

"Will you dance?" he asked. He swallowed past the golf ball sized lump in his throat. This was worse than the very first time he'd ever asked her to dance. It seemed that every single pair of eyes in the entire village was now focussed on them.

"Dance?" Cassie looked around. His friends were behind him but she didn't give them any more attention than anyone else in the room. Ben could only imagine them all falling about laughing at him. "With you?"

"Yes." Ben forced the word out between gritted teeth. He couldn't give up now otherwise he would never hear the end of it. "Me and you. Dance together."

"No," she said so softly, he strained to hear her over the vibrating disco music. "I don't think that's a great idea."

He leant down, putting his lips near her ear. "It's not a great idea, no. But if you don't dance with me I'll be forced to see if Little Ed has got a photo of you in those handcuffs he can put on the front page of next week's paper."

Cassie gasped. "You wouldn't."

"I would," he assured her. "We need to dance together."

He put out his hand. Her eyes narrowed, her confusion showing even as she took his hand and allowed him to lead her onto the dance floor.

"Why are you doing this?" She whispered.

"I have to." He wished she wasn't so close all he could smell was the fruity shampoo she still used. The sweet smell tantalised him even after he drew himself up to his full height.

The music changed and the soft strains of a popular love song filled the room. Ben tried to hold in a heartfelt groan. Could this get any worse? It was bad enough he was there in the middle of the room with the whole village looking on with barely disguised interest without the music demanding he hold Cassie close.

"Let's get it over with," Cassie said with a lack of enthusiasm that matched his own. "Then I expect both you and Little Ed to promise to destroy any pictorial evidence there may be."

"Gladly," Ben agreed while hoping his body didn't do anything to betray how much he would like to keep a photo of Cassie in handcuffs.

Her arms looped around his back, settling at the top of his belt. He reluctantly put his around her, the material of her dress smooth and satiny against his fingers.

Three minutes. Three minutes the song would last. He could do this.

Ben closed his eyes hoping his hands wouldn't slide down the soft fabric. He was barely holding it together while his hands were splayed over her back. If they slid down then he would definitely be in trouble. Every fibre of his being wanted to let his hands cup her round bottom and pull her hips in to nestle against his.

Right at that moment, Ben couldn't remember why sending her off to follow her dream had been such a great idea when he didn't want the song to ever end. He never wanted to let her go again.

Chapter Four

Cassie's hands rested lightly on Ben's belt, his large hands warm against her back. She wished she hadn't worn such a blatantly sexy dress—dungarees would've been better. Though, if she was honest with herself, she'd worn it because she wanted to show Ben what he'd lost.

The long buried desire to find out why exactly he'd dumped her surfaced. The old hurt and sense of betrayal burned in her gut. Over the years, she'd never been able to work it out. Ben had simply told her that he didn't love her any more but intuition told her there was a lot more to it than that. It was long past time to find out the truth.

She wiggled a little nearer. A muscle in Ben's back stiffened and he tried to pull away but Cassie tightened her grip on his belt. Although he'd said his feelings for her were gone, sexually there had been nothing wrong in their relationship. And judging by the bulge in his pants he was still attracted to her.

Cassie swayed her hips in time to the music, watching the telltale muscle in his jaw jump as he tried to keep himself under control.

"Something wrong?" she asked, blinking innocently.

"What the hell are you doing?" he responded through gritted teeth.

"Dancing."

"You're gyrating."

"Am not," Cassie grinned up at him, moving her hips in a

circle against his erection. "That's gyrating."

"Crap!"

"You know," she continued. "We could probably carry on with this later."

"Later?"

"Yes, later," she purred. "Just me and you. For old time's sake."

"Not a good idea."

"Why not?" Cassie slid one hand under his T-shirt and trailed a finger across his waist. "I can see you haven't brought a plus one with you, so there's no girlfriend to stop you."

"I..."

"And I can tell you want to." She would find out why he sent her off to London if it killed her. But making love with Ben, reviving all the feelings she'd tried so hard to forget, just might finish her off.

"We can't." Ben shook his head, clearly trying to regain control of himself while his body told her a different story. "It would be an awful idea."

"I think I have a spare set of handcuffs. Maybe we could put those to some use?"

He closed his eyes and Cassie knew exactly what was going through his mind. And it certainly wasn't him using industrial strength cutters to get her free from underneath her work desk.

"Walk out," he hissed, pulling her in front of him and giving her a little shove in the back. "Get outside."

His tone wasn't exactly friendly and a small frisson of unease skittered up her spine. Maybe getting him all overheated hadn't been such a great idea.

She smiled as she left the village hall, trying not to look intimidated or aware of the knowing glances of her friends and neighbours as they left together.

Ben took hold of her hand and they walked to the rear of the building.

He pointed at the wooden bench. "Sit."

Cassie followed his demands even as her heart squeezed painfully. How could it be that after all this time she still loved him?

"Why?"

Even in the dim light, Cassie could see the tortured look in his grey eyes. Anger kicked in and overrode her upset.

"Why what? Dancing together was your idea, remember?"

He pulled a hand through his hair. "It was to settle a score."

"Really?" Cassie injected as much scorn into the word as she could manage. "Some sort of stupid macho bet?"

Ben sighed. "Something like that."

She blinked as hurt won the battle of her emotions. "That's all I'm worth to you?"

"No!" He sat beside her, pulling one of her hands into both of his. His thumb trailed a lazy pattern over the delicate bones in her wrist. "You're everything to me."

His words stunned her and for a moment she was certain she'd heard him wrongly.

"I'm everything to you?"

He looked skywards as though he regretted saying the telling words. Finally he looked back at her, the way he'd always looked at her before he broke things off between them, the love evident on his face.

His head dipped. He was going to kiss her. She shivered slightly as his lips touched hers, despite it being a warm summer evening. The kiss was familiar, yet new, and her body reacted immediately. She'd told herself she hadn't missed him. He was simply her first love, the only boy to have kissed her and that was why she'd pined for him.

After she'd left, she'd kissed a good few more men before she'd admitted to herself that no one kissed quite like Ben. And he wasn't simply her teenage crush all grown up—he was the only man she was ever going to love with such fervour it sometimes scared her.

Even now, as she kissed him back, those scary feelings were returning. She shouldn't have come back because she looked set to let history repeat itself. He'd told her he didn't want her once. Why was she putting herself through it all over again?

Cassie pulled away, putting a hand on the broad expanse of his chest. "I can't do this again. You broke my heart once and I left because I couldn't bear to stay. I'm sorry, I was wrong. I need to ..."

"You left because I finished things between us?" He sounded as though that was the first time he'd ever considered such a notion. Of course that's why she left. She'd been expecting him to propose when she came back from Uni, but instead he'd broken things off.

"Why else, Ben?"

"You had that job offer. You were going to leave anyway."

"Wait." Cassie pulled her hand away and stood up, putting as much distance between them as she could. "I told you about that job offer because we shared everything. I was never going to take it."

"But it was your dream, you were so excited." He shook his head as though trying to clear his ears. "You wanted to be a journalist at a national paper in London. That's what you worked for."

"I can write stories anywhere," Cassie turned away as whoops and shouts of joy came from the village hall. Inside, Lizzie and Nick were starting their lives together while hers was shattering all over again. "I wanted to stay and help you on the farm more than I ever wanted to leave."

"You don't belong here." His voice was harsh but Cassie heard the thread of despair laced through his words.

"So you sent me away?" She hardly dared ask the question but she needed to know the answer.

"Yes." The single word seemed to be ripped from his throat.

"That wasn't your decision to make. We should have made it together."

"I thought if you stayed you would regret it. Farm life is hardly easy. You needed to follow your dream."

"And you needed to treat me as though I was capable of making my own decisions." Cassie whirled around, pointing a finger at him. "This is the twenty first century. How dare you presume to tell me how to live my life?"

"It wasn't like that." Ben pushed up from the bench and walked towards her. "I did it because I love you. I wanted you to be free."

"Don't," she held out a hand and he stopped. Cassie closed herself off to the devastation obvious in Ben's face. "Your nobility broke my heart."

"Cassie, please, I thought I was doing the right thing."

"If you'd ever known me at all, you would've known that what you did was the wrong thing. The most wrong thing." Tears fell down her cheeks but she tried to hold back the wracking sobs threatening to break loose. "Stay away from me."

She took off her high heels and ran towards the lane. How dare he make a decision for her that had changed the course of her life? They should be married now with a couple of babies. She definitely shouldn't be running home with her shoes in her hand like a teenager caught out after curfew.

Chapter Five

Ben headed towards the newspaper office. It was the middle of the day and people were milling about, doing their shopping and stopping to chat on the narrow pavements.

His stomach knotted as he noticed Mrs Cromaty across the road. She raised a hand in greeting and a knowing eyebrow. The whole of the village would know in two minutes flat that after their spat the previous evening Ben was going to smooth things over. Or so they thought.

Ben had actually watched and waited until Cassie left the newspaper office before he'd approached. What he was about to do was something he didn't want her to have any knowledge of until he was ready.

He took a folded sheet of paper out of his jeans pocket as he entered the building. She was either going to think he was certifiable or love him forever. Whichever way it went, he was going to be the laughing stock of the village for goodness only knew how long.

"I'd like to place an advertisement in this week's paper." Ben announced.

"What type of advert?"

Ben was glad the owner of the paper stood the other side of the counter and not his irritating son. He wasn't sure he could handle going through with his plan if he had to face Little Ed.

"Um ..." Ben gulped down his nerves. *Faint heart never won fair maid.* If he wanted Cassie in his life, permanently, he had to do this. He had to show her how sorry he was and the only way he could think to do that was humiliate himself. Completely. But she was totally worth it. "I guess in the lonely hearts column. Do you have one of those?"

Mr Swales eyed him suspiciously. "I would think a box of chocolates and a bunch of nice flowers would sort things out with Cassie. Has to be simpler than a lonely hearts advert."

"I'm not sure chocolate and flowers are the way to Cassie's heart."

Mr Swales snorted through his nose. "And advertising for a girlfriend in the paper she works at is?"

"Maybe if you read what I'd like you to print you can decide where it should be best placed?" Ben had agonised for hours over the words he'd scrawled on the paper he handed to Mr Swales. They would decide his future—his and Cassie's.

Mr Swales looked at the words, then back to Ben, his shaggy eyebrows rising to meet his receding hairline. "Really? You really want me to put exactly this into the paper?"

"Yes, I really do." He spoke quickly before he could change his mind. "You think it will work?"

"Who knows, son. But it will certainly give everyone a laugh."

"Great, you'll send me the bill?" Ben backed out of the office, Mr Swales's reply lost in the cacophony of laughter that followed him as he hurried away.

Oh God. What had he done?

Chapter Six

A week later, four days after the newspaper had been printed and distributed throughout the village, Ben had about given up on hearing from Cassie. His master plan at gaining her forgiveness had failed.

He picked up the folded paper from the counter in the milking shed. His own words stared back at him:

Lonely farmer seeks journalist who holds the key to his heart with a view to a permanent relationship. Apologises unreservedly for past arrogance and promises to have learnt from mistake.

He couldn't go anywhere without fingers pointed at him and people sniggering behind their hands. And that was just the polite ones. He'd achieved utter humiliation but Cassie remained silent.

"Ben!"

He looked up at the shout of his name, taking time to let the cow he'd milked loose into the main pen. He would let her back out to the field when he'd dealt with the interruption.

Cassie strode through the milking shed, the heels of her boots clipping against the concrete floor.

"You've seen the paper then?"

He deserved whatever she wanted to throw at him. She was right. He'd been a high handed arrogant fool. His only defence was he'd been young then. Young and incredibly stupid. He'd never make that mistake now.

"Yes, I have. And I have an advert of my own." Her eyes were bright as she smiled directly at him. The nervous swirling in his gut dissipated somewhat. "Read this."

He took the paper she offered and scanned the headline before looking back to her.

"Read it!" She urged.

Ben's eyes followed the words but he couldn't make sense of it. He understood that she'd written an article she hoped would go into the local newspaper but what she'd written wasn't right.

"Cassie, I don't ..."

"What do you think?" She smiled, her enthusiasm infectious even as his brain struggled to process the information.

"I'm not sure you being here all the time would be such a great idea." Ben searched for the right thing to say. "You'd be a distraction."

"I would bloody well hope so!"

"But why would you want to do this?"

"Because I love you, you stupid man." She stepped forward and took the sheet of paper from his hand. "Your mum and I talked about using the old barn as a bed and breakfast cottage for holidaying families. I guess she always thought I would do it when we got married."

"She never said." Ben looked away from Cassie towards the village and the graveyard in St Peter's Church where his mother rested next to his father. "Why didn't she tell me your plans?"

"I think everyone simply expected us to get married and maybe she never thought she had to tell you about every single conversation we ever had. Maybe she meant to but there was never enough time?"

Cassie rubbed a hand over his forearm, the gesture comforting but her nearness robbed him of his ability to think logically. His mother had died after a three month struggle against a particularly aggressive form of cancer. He hated that he hadn't known his mother's plans before she died.

"She told me I should follow my heart." Ben swept an arm around the farm. "And I did. I stayed on the farm. I've done everything I can to keep it going."

She faltered at his words, taking a small step backwards. "You've done a good job. Your parents would be proud."

"But I've been too proud to see exactly what my mum meant. I'd already sent you away when she died. I thought I needed to make a success of myself before I could ever think of coming after you and begging you to come back. I wanted there to be something for you to come back to."

"There was you," she whispered. "I would've come back for you."

"But you've lived in a big city, had a great salary." He looked at her clothes. He could probably keep the farm going for a month with the money her outfit had cost. "I couldn't expect you to come home to nothing."

"Then you underestimate me." She waved the paper in his face. "Again."

"It takes money to get a business up and running. I don't have that kind of money." He hardly dared hope there was a chance of them making it work. And yet, he would do anything to ensure she never left his side again.

"I do. It's called a redundancy package. And as your wife, my money would be your money. Your struggles would be mine."

"My wife?" Ben repeated the words as a denial sprang to his lips. "But you're not ..."

"Ben," she said patiently as though she were talking to a particularly difficult child. "I'm not your wife because you haven't asked me."

"You'd want to marry me even after I've acted like such an idiot?" He indicated the paper she still held. "And you'd really run a bed and breakfast here to help the farm stay afloat?"

"Haven't I already written the article to let people know that's what we'll be doing here? Haven't I already contacted some of my old colleagues to make sure they'll write a nice Sunday feature about the popularity of farm holidays for families?"

"I don't deserve you," he mumbled against her hair.

"You're right," Cassie agreed. "You don't."

"What can I do to make it up to you?"

"You can spend the rest of your life showing me how very sorry you are."

Her mischievous grin told him all he needed to know. He didn't know why or how but she'd forgiven him—she truly loved him.

"You won't get bored here? Want to run off back to the big city?" He had to ask the question.

She shook her head. "I can think of more exciting adventures I can have right here."

"Like what?"

She whispered something in his ear that made him want to pick her up and haul her off inside caveman style.

"I love you." For now, he settled for kissing the tip of her nose. "And I promise I'll spend every day for the rest of my life showing you."

And he did.

About the author:

Catherine Coles has written stories since the day she could form sentences! Being a member of the wonderfully supportive Minxes of Romance has encouraged her to follow her dreams with an extra burst of passion. Catherine writes medical romance with a focus on modern, sassy heroines and the sexy, successful heroes who enrich their lives. Catherine lives in the north east of England where, as a foster carer, she currently shares her home with six children, two spoiled pooches and a cat who thinks she's a dog!

Hot, Bothered and Bewitched

Kat French

Chapter One

Old habits die hard.

Seraphine Mansfield knelt on the bare floorboards of her dining room and arranged two long, silk ribbons into triangles in front of her, one ribbon laid over the other to form a six-point star. With any luck, the rest of her furniture would arrive in the morning, but for now the empty dining room lent itself perfectly to a little magic.

She eyed her handiwork critically, then carefully placed a votive candle on each point of the star. Six in total, three pink and three red. Pink for romance, red for hot romance. As she lit them one by one, working from West to East, she offered up words of reverence to the evening star, old enchantments learned at her mother's knee.

She picked up the small silver scissors from her spell box and snipped off one of her own black curls from beneath her hairline at the back, feeling around to make sure it wouldn't show. The idea of being quizzed about her hacked-off haircut by her new neighbours had her ruffling her curls anxiously into place. This had better work. She placed the small lock of hair in the centre of the triangle carefully.

For the most part, Seraphine had managed to shake off her wiccan roots as she'd put herself through vet school, but if there was ever an occasion likely to send her back to her grandmother's spell book, it was this. Her thirtieth birthday, all alone in a new village without so much as a pet budgie for company. She travelled without companions. A black cat would have been way too clichéd, and she saw enough animals during the day to be happy to close her door to them in the evenings.

Besides, Coombethwaite was supposed to be a fresh start, a place where no one knew her or any of her eccentric female relatives. Her grandmother was practically folklore royalty back home in Devon, and her mother and aunts were happily following in her footsteps. It wasn't that Seraphine was embarrassed or scornful of her heritage, she'd just chosen a different path in life. Or she was trying to, at least. She wanted to be normal, whatever that was, and as a lifelong animal lover, a career as a vet had seemed the perfect choice. So what if she gave the occasional sick animal a little extra help that medicine couldn't offer? Where was the harm in that?

What she really yearned for was a family of her own, an adoring husband, round limbed babies with bouncing black curls like their mother. That wasn't so big an ask, was it?

Except putting her theory into practice was proving harder than she'd ever imagined. It seemed she had a knack for picking the wrong men, as evidenced by David, the potential latest love interest in Seraphine's life to make a hasty stage-left exit after meeting her unconventional family.

It was fast becoming a familiar pattern, so she'd jumped at the chance to take over from the retiring vet in a lakeside village where she could start with a clean slate. It was far from home, and all the more tantalising for it.

Except for times like now, when she found herself alone with a bottle of Champagne on Halloween. It was her birthday, and the most magical night of the year, and she wasn't above casting a little love spell in an effort to draw the perfect man towards her. Desperate times, desperate measures. She'd had enough of ready meals for one and a bed that felt too big.

She jumped as someone rapped on the front door of her little cottage, her concentration broken before she'd barely settled in.

Typical. She couldn't even cast a tiny spell in peace. The incantation was supposed to conjure up her true love within twenty-eight days, but only if she could cast it properly. Was this mother nature's way of telling her to give in, that she was a lost cause destined to live alone forever?

"Anyone home?"

A raised male voice came through the door as her caller banged again.

Seraphine dragged her hair up with a band from the pocket of her robe and sighed. Not answering wasn't an option, her lamp was on in the tiny front lounge and she'd laid a crackling fire in the grate. The last thing she wanted was to start life in the village with a reputation as stand-offish. She dragged back the old bolt on the front door and swung it wide.

"You're not Harold Mahoney," the stranger said.

Seraphine eyed the tousle haired man on her doorstep, momentarily taken aback by his chocolate penny eyes and the full cupid's bow of his mouth. Hmm. She glanced up at the night sky in surprise. Even for a Mansfield witch, that was mighty quick work. Twenty eight days? More like twenty eight seconds…

"There's nothing wrong with your powers of observation, is there?" She gave herself a mental shake, concentrating her attentions back to the vision in front of her. Harold Mahoney, the outgoing village vet, had been six foot two and thick set with a penchant for Arran sweaters, a far cry from Seraphine's five foot four frame, which was currently wrapped in a floor-length black fluffy bathrobe and nothing else.

Mystery man's eyes registered surprised amusement, and then he yowled and his mouth twisted in annoyance.

"Enough, cat!"

Seraphine glanced down as he unzipped his battered leather jacket, and then watched with startled eyes as he unhooked a large black cat's claws from where they'd embedded themselves into the neck of his T-shirt.

"Tell me you're the new vet?" He fished the cat out of his coat. "Because this cat needs somewhere to crash, and it's sure as hell's not gonna be my house."

"You don't like cats?"

"I don't like this cat." Seraphine followed his gaze and studied the creature. In truth, it wasn't the best looking feline specimen. He appeared to have lost an eye somewhere on his travels, and one of his ears had seen better days. He was an old soldier all right, and he didn't look all that happy with his predicament.

"Whose is he?" Seraphine wrapped her arms around her slender frame against the chilled evening air.

"No idea. Who are you?"

"I'm Harold Mahoney's replacement." She saw his brows twitch with interest. "Who are you?"

"Isaac Quinn. Cat rescuer, farrier, and local fireman."

"That's quite a list."

He shrugged. "I'm a man of many talents."

"You're also a man who's bleeding."

Seraphine gestured towards the angry scratch that ran from his neck to his collarbone, currently seeping blood into the edge of his T-shirt.

"Bloody cat!" He touched a hand to the wound and looked at his blood-damp fingers, and the sour-faced puss took his cue and escaped from Isaac's clutches. He lunged to catch it, but needn't have bothered. The cat turned and shot him a hiss, then sauntered past Seraphine's legs with an investigatory rub and disappeared into the cottage.

Looking considerably happier without his encumbrance, Isaac craned his neck for Seraphine's attention. "Am I likely to die, do you think?"

She rolled her eyes. "You better come in and clean that up. I have some cream."

"Your new cat won't be pleased to see me," Isaac muttered, throwing a sour glance at the cat, who'd stretched out on the rug in front of the fire. "The vet can hardly turn away an animal in need, and all…"

"I'm not officially the village's new vet until Monday morning," Seraphine pointed out as she closed the front door and gestured for him to sit down on the small couch by the fire. "I'll get my first aid box."

The candles around the ribboned star still burned on the dining room floor, and she blew them out hastily, glancing back towards the living room door. God! The idea that Isaac Quinn might have seen her little love altar made her palms sweat.

No one here knows. I'm okay. She snatched up the ribbons and candles and stuffed them into the sideboard with a sigh of relief.

She retrieved the first aid box from the back of the kitchen cupboard, and returned to the lounge to find Isaac had removed his jacket and flung it over the arm of the sofa.

She paused, her fingers curled around the shawl collar of her robe. There was a drop dead gorgeous man in her living room, and a cold bottle of champagne on the table. She'd planned to drink it alone with a good movie, but the prospect had somehow lost its appeal.

He glanced down at the first aid box as she perched next to him, taking care to make sure her robe folded over her knees.

"Are you going to hurt me?"

"Well, I'm used to patients who can't answer back, so quite possibly."

"Maybe I need anesthetic first, then…" his mischievous eyes slipped to the unopened champagne bottle, then back to hers.

"Are you always such a wimp?"

"I'm a fireman. That makes me officially macho."

Seraphine flipped open the tin lid and rooted through it for antiseptic and cotton wool. "Good. Keep still then."

She tipped a little of the cold liquid out onto the cotton wool, then looked across and studied him. How best to do this? It was a deep scratch, it needed a thorough clean. She moved around and knelt next to him, then angled her head to demonstrate what he should do. "Tip your head, like this?"

He did as instructed and exposed the strong column of his neck for her ministrations.

Seraphine chewed her top lip, suddenly nervous at the thought of touching him. The firelight cast a golden glow over his skin, rendering him sultry despite the dried blood. Tentatively, she reached out and stroked the dampened cotton wool down his wound, clearing away the blood to properly reveal the deep scratch below.

"Well, nurse?" he muttered out the side of his mouth and tried to look at her from the corner of his eye.

"Keep still." She worked to make sure she removed all of the blood from the wound. His skin was warm beneath her fingers, and she could feel the flicker of his pulse at the base of his throat. Was it racing, slightly? Job done, she let out the breath she hadn't realized she'd been holding and returned her attention to the tin box. Somewhere in there was a tub of her grandmother's handmade cream, a special cure-all tincture. When she looked up again she found Isaac studying her.

"You didn't tell me your name," he said softly.

"It's Seraphine."

His eyebrows lifted, acknowledgement of her name's unusualness. "And is there a Mr. Seraphine?"

She turned to look at the cat. "Looks like there is now."

She didn't miss the interested flare in Isaac's eyes before she glanced down and unscrewed the lid on the cream. She scooped a little onto her fingers.

"Can you…?" She instinctively reached out her other hand and gently turned his chin away from her again. He closed his eyes, and his five o'clock shadow bristled beneath her fingers. She swallowed hard as a shiver of attraction slipped down her spine.

"Just so you know, I'm attached, too." She couldn't see his face, but she felt his jaw widen into a smile. "Dulcie slobbers her food and has evil drool, but I'm devoted."

The cool cream dissolved into his skin on contact, yet still Seraphine took her time to slowly massage it in.

His neck was firm, and her fingers followed the length of his collarbone until they met the barrier of his T-shirt. His eyes were still closed when she glanced up at his profile, and for a second, she let her hands rest on him. Or to be more accurate, she couldn't take her hands, or her eyes, off him. He was a complete stranger, yet in that moment, she felt she'd known him for her whole lifetime.

"All done," she said eventually, and busied herself packing away the supplies whilst she regained her composure. Her fingers lingered on something lying at the bottom of the tin.

"I'll give you nine out of ten for your bedside manner, Veterinary."

"What did I lose a point on?" Seraphine drew herself up to standing.

Isaac shrugged and shot her a lop-sided grin. "I'm not in bed."

She looked at him. He looked at her. She slipped the packet from the tin into her pocket.

"Would you like a glass of champagne? It's my birthday."

Chapter Two

Isaac watched Seraphine retreat into the back of the cottage in search of another glass. He appreciated the gentle sway of her hips, and the graceful curve of her neck revealed by the way she'd haphazardly tied up her dark curls.

It had been a while. He wasn't even sure he was fit for sex, the accident had left him weakened on one side, but Jesus, this woman was something else. From the second she'd opened her door and fixed him with her big, violet eyes, he'd felt it. That fizz of mutual attraction, that magical sizzle of anticipation.

He glanced at the cat, and found it watching him with its one good eye. Isaac shrugged. "Okay, okay. I forgive you. Just no more funny stuff, right?"

The cat huffed and made a show of closing his eye, then rolled away from Isaac to bake its belly before the warmth of the fire.

Isaac scrubbed his hand over his chin, glad for once that eagle-eyed Mrs. Cromaty had called him out. She was a thorn in the side of Coombethwaite's retained fire brigade, always calling on them for tenuous reasons. Tonight's stray cat hadn't really been his jurisdiction; they usually palmed stray cats off on Drew, their resident cat-whisperer, but Enid was a neighbor and he'd felt obliged when she'd knocked on his door. He thanked his lucky stars now though. It might even warrant a bunch of flowers.

His stint with the fire brigade was all a long way from his years as a farrier for the Household Cavalry Mounted Regiment, but his days as a Lance Corporal were ancient history now. Stupid really. He'd managed two tours of duty without major incident or injury, only to be put out of the army by a rogue kick from an angry stallion. He'd lost more than his career after the accident twelve months ago. He'd lost his place in the world, and the woman he'd planned to marry. Turned out she was more in love with the idea of being a military wife than she was with him.

He was single, and lonely, and a little bit broken, but this suddenly felt like a night to take chances.

Chapter Three

Seraphine placed the second glass down next to hers on the coffee table and handed the bottle to Isaac to uncork.

"Remind me again. Fireman, cat-rescuer, and what?"

Isaac expertly uncorked the champagne and filled up their glasses. "Farrier."

"Fireman and farrier? You like to play with fire, I take it?"

She noticed the shadow that flickered across his face, and his slight wince as he stretched to place the bottle on the table. "You don't enjoy your work?"

"It's not that. I've been…" he sighed heavily and lounged back against the sofa. "I've been out of action for a while."

Seraphine heard the unspoken melancholy behind his ambiguous words and chose not to pry. She had her secrets; he was more than entitled to his.

"So. You were a Halloween baby, then." He reached out and touched the rim of his glass against hers formally. "And very bewitching you are, too. Happy Birthday."

"Thank you." She smiled softly and sipped her wine, enjoying the cool fizz, the warm fire and the unexpected good company. On the rug, her other new acquaintance flinched his paws in his sleep.

"I could take you to the King's Head to celebrate, if you like?"

Isaac toyed idly with the end of Seraphine's belt as she curled her legs up beneath her. She watched his fingers for a second. He had the sort of hands you'd expect of a farrier. Strong, capable, a little bashed.

"Or we could just stay here by the fire and drink champagne," she said.

"I like your plan better."

She couldn't be certain, but he seemed a smidge closer than he'd been a second or two ago.

"I could wash the blood out of your T-shirt for you, if you like."

He looked at her for a few silent, assessing seconds, then handed her his glass to hold. "I'd like that very much."

Seraphine's breath caught in her throat as he reached for the hem of his faded T-shirt and peeled it unhurriedly over his head.

Christ. The way his clothes clung to his body had hinted he was in good condition, but bare-chested in the firelight, he was beyond that. He was beautiful.

She handed back his glass, and he drank deeply. She refilled them both, and moved a little closer as she settled back down.

"You're a definite improvement on Harold Mahoney." Isaac reached out and worked her hair free of its band with gentle fingers. She closed her eyes for a second and enjoyed the pleasurable pressure of his fingers as he massaged the back of her neck.

"I don't do things like this, Isaac." She turned her face and touched her lips against the pulse point on his wrist.

"Good. Me neither." He stroked the back of his fingers along her jaw. "So, you're a vet, huh?"

She nodded, trying not to be distracted as he smoothed her hair behind her ear and rubbed the lobe slowly between his thumb and forefinger.

"I like healing things." She swallowed a good glug of champagne and glanced at the cat, knowing she had work to do there. "And you're a fireman, huh?"

"I like saving things." He looked at the cat too, but the expression on his face was far less charitable. "Aren't we just a regular pair of super heroes? The good people of Coombethwaite can sleep safer in their beds tonight."

"Will you sleep with me in my bed tonight, Isaac?" Seraphine heard the vulnerability in her own voice.

He tugged on her belt gently in answer, drawing her against him.

"Are you sure?" His eyes searched hers, and then his lashes swept down as he dipped his head to kiss her. He tasted of champagne and smelled of warm spice, and his kiss melted every rational thought in her head. His fingers cradled her jaw as he opened his mouth to deepen the kiss, sliding up the scale from sensual to erotic to knee-trembling as his tongue moved languidly over hers. Seraphine let her hands explore the contours of his chest, firm and warmed by the fire. His nipples stiffened beneath her palms, and he groaned and sank his teeth into the softness of her lower lip when her fingers skimmed his belt buckle.

"Strictly speaking, it's your turn to take something off." He nibbled along her lip, a tiny line of sensual bites.

"But I'm naked under my robe."

He pulled his head back a fraction and raised his eyebrows. "I think I love you."

"Aah, but will you respect me in the morning?"

"Yes. Take your robe off."

Seraphine paused for a second. It wasn't nerves. Something about Isaac felt too entirely right for nerves to have any place in the tiny living room. It was a desire to go slow, because you can only have your first time with someone once.

"Take it off for me?"

He laughed softly and pushed his hand through his hair, then placed both of their glasses down on the coffee table.

"Seraphine."

It was the first time he'd said her name, and no one else in her life had come close to saying it in such a sexy way before.

He reached for her belt and worked the knot open.

Seraphine felt it loosen, but Isaac didn't rush to remove it. Maybe he took it easy for her benefit, or perhaps he yearned to make the moment last, too. Either way, she wanted him all the more fiercely for it.

She took a deep breath, and shrugged the robe off her shoulders, clutching it loosely with one hand to prevent it from sliding down altogether.

Isaac leaned in close and kissed her shoulder, then trailed his warm mouth across her collarbone. He paused to pay special attention to the sensitive hollow at the base of her throat, then drifted across to kiss her other shoulder. At the same time his hand moved to cover hers, and he unfurled her grip on the robe and let it fall.

She saw the way he swallowed hard, and admired him for looking up into her eyes rather than down at her bared breasts.

"It feels more like my birthday than yours," he murmured, sliding his hand around the back of her neck and pulling her in until her breasts brushed against the solid wall of his chest. A tiny sigh of pleasure bubbled in Seraphine's throat, and her nipples hardened in reaction to his nearness.

"No…" She gasped a little as his hands moved up to cup the fullness of her breasts. "You're definitely the best birthday present I've ever had."

His thumbs circled her nipples as he laughed softly into her mouth. "Consider the cat my gift to you."

Seraphine's fingers moved to stroke the peach soft, faded denim that covered his straining crotch. "I don't know. I think you may have something else I'd like."

Never in her entire life had she been so brazen, but then never in her entire life had she been so turned on, either.

Isaac let her get as far as opening his belt and popping his top button before he caught her wrist. "Come here." He pulled her onto his lap, leaving the robe behind her on the sofa. This time he didn't hesitate about looking at her body. His gaze moved hungrily over every inch of her, and she let him take his fill. When he finally lifted his eyes to hers again, lust had darkened them from milk chocolate to black coffee, and the expression in them told her how much he liked what he saw.

"I've never seen anyone as beautiful as you, Seraphine."

His words were shot through with sincerity, and Sophie nestled into his lap. She could feel his very physical confirmation of her effect on him, but something else drew her attention, too. A heat only she'd be able to detect radiated from his thigh, the kind of heat that innately warned her of injury, or pain. Something had happened to this man, something that had caused him great distress. Tuning into him, she detected a deep ache, both in his body and his heart. Isaac was walking wounded, just as she was, and in that moment she wanted only to take those feelings away for him. For both of them.

When he bent his head to the swell of her breasts and drew first one pebble-hard nub and then the other into his mouth, something inside Seraphine snapped. She went from wanting to take it slow to wanting him desperately, to being drenched in desire for him. She straddled his hips, and moaned with appreciation when his hands swept down her spine to caress her bottom.

Isaac responded to her increase in tempo like-for-like. His mouth and hands were everywhere, and she hollowed her spine and arched against his chest when he finally gave her what she needed. His sure, sensitive touch between her legs made her body clench and her breath catch in her throat, and he kissed her through it as he stroked her towards orgasm. His tongue slid into her mouth, and Seraphine reached for her robe, remembering the packet she'd rescued from the first aid box earlier.

"What's wrong?" he whispered, as his deft fingers made her all but yelp.

"There's a condom in the pocket of my robe."

She felt low laughter rumble through his chest as he found

the foil wrapper.

"Will you marry me, Seraphine?"

"That depends." She unbuttoned his jeans and pushed them down, and he managed to free himself from all of his clothing within seconds.

"On what?" he breathed heavily as Seraphine's hand encircled his rigid erection.

She rested her forehead on his. "Love me, love my cat."

He paused for a second. "It's a big ask. He's a brute."

Seraphine smiled, then gasped, suddenly unable to speak as he touched her in a way that was beyond erotic. "Isaac…" she breathed, letting him know how close he had her.

"I know, baby," he gentled her with his mouth and his words before he ripped the foil packet with his teeth and sheathed himself.

Seraphine sensed that this position was good for him, and loved that she could give him pleasure without causing him pain. She held her breath as he positioned himself, and closed her eyes as she sank down onto every heavenly inch of him.

His eyelids were half closed with lust when she opened hers again, and he blew out a low, shaky breath of pleasure as she began to move slowly on him. His hands encircled her waist, his thumbs massaging her rib cage as his eyes roved over her breasts.

"Much as I'd like it to, this isn't going to last long," he breathed, and as he put his hand between her thighs Seraphine's body responded to his warning. She clung to Isaac's broad shoulders and surrendered to the sensations that wracked her body, holding him tight as his release roared out of him too. They were connected. Physically. Cerebrally. Completely.

Chapter Four

"Wow." Seraphine loosened her vice-like grip on Isaac's shoulders.

"Back atcha, lady." His hands stroked her as her breathing slowly returned to somewhere approaching normal. "I'll upgrade you to a ten for your bedside manner."

She smiled into his neck. "Stay with me tonight?"

"As long as you can promise the cat won't kill me."

Seraphine eyed the sleeping, black fur ball. "I think you're safe." She climbed off Isaac's lap and reached for her robe. He eased himself to the edge of the sofa and placed a slow, tender kiss against her hipbone.

"Happy Birthday, Seraphine."

She smoothed a hand over the silk of his dark hair, then wrapped her arms around him as he stood. His arms cocooned her, a warm circle every bit as powerful as the votive circles her mother lived her life by.

"Go on upstairs," she murmured. "I'll lock up and be right there."

In the kitchen, Seraphine placed the glasses in the sink and reached down to fuss the cat's head when he followed her in search of food. As she placed a saucer of chicken on the floor, he eyed it with disdain and jumped up onto the kitchen table and meowed loudly. Seraphine frowned. She'd owned enough cats over the years to know that chicken should be a sure-fire hit. She looked at him quizzically, and as she did so, she noticed the envelope beneath his paw.

It had arrived yesterday, and she'd recognized her mother's bright cerise fountain pen ink instantly. She'd intended to open it earlier, but Isaac had well and truly sidetracked her. A glance at the clock confirmed it was still her birthday, just. She eased the envelope from beneath the cat's paw and ripped it open.

Job done, the big black kitty jumped down instantly and crossed to his bowl to wolf down the chicken.

#

Seraphine opened the kitchen door with the envelope in her hand, and stepped outside for a second to drink in the clear, cold night and the glittering stars that hung over Coombe Mountain. Everything was still, and a sparkle of frost had decorated the garden, a last unexpected birthday gift from Mother Nature. Opening the birthday card, a tiny dark curl of hair tied with a red ribbon tumbled out into her palm.

'Your first curl, my darling! I cast the twenty-eight day spell on it just for you, I don't like to think of you alone up there in the wilds on your Birthday!

Call me soon, love Mum xx'

Seraphine laughed softly and shook her head. Who knew if her own spell had conjured Isaac, or if her mother's spell had?

For a girl who'd turned her back on magic, it had been a bewitching evening of black cats, magic spells, and birthday wishes that really did come true.

Seraphine tipped a wink at Venus as she stepped back inside the cottage and locked the door. There was a fireman in her bedroom, and she was feeling distinctly hot and bothered...

About the author:

Kat French is a self-confessed romance junkie, daydreamer and champion wine drinker. She writes sexy romantic comedy, and lives in England with her husband and their two little boys.

Kat also writes erotic romance under the pen name Kitty French. You can find Kat on twitter @KatFrench_

And her blog is www.katfrench.co.uk

Kat's Books
Undertaking Love

Kitty's Books
Knight & Play (Erotic Romance Series)
Knight & Stay (Erotic Romance Series Book 2)
Knight & Day coming December 2013.
Wanderlust.

Lighting Love's Spark

Sally Clements

Chapter One

Give me a reason not to kill you.

Annabel Jackson smiled, slipped a napkin between the pages and closed her new paperback. There would be time to read after breakfast—letting her sausage sandwich go cold wasn't an option.

A passing waitress offered a top-up from a glass coffee jug, and Annabel gratefully accepted.

In a few short months, so much had changed. She drank coffee rather than cappuccino, ate sausages for breakfast on Saturday mornings rather than muesli. Best of all, she could indulge in reading the latest WD Daniels without supercilious comments from across the table.

She chewed a mouthful of sausage sandwich, then picked up her book and continued reading. *Harper never lied, and something about his cold stare...*

"Daddy! That's her, that's Teacher!"

As the only teacher from Coombethwaite Primary in Tina's Café, it was a fair bet that the new arrivals were talking about her. With a quiet sigh, she replaced the napkin between the pages and looked up.

Six-year-old Chloe Walker stood before her table. Long brown plaits hung either side of her slender face, and she wriggled on the spot like an over-excited puppy. Her blue eyes were open as wide as they could possibly be, and her smile cut deep dimples into her cheeks.

"Hi, Teacher." Chloe tugged on the hand of the tall man she held captive. "Daddy, this is Teacher."

"Good morning, Chloe." Annabel resisted the urge to grab the napkin from her book and dab at the corners of her mouth. If she was covered in sauce, so be it. She glanced up. "Good morning, Mr Walker…"

Annabel's mouth dried at the first glimpse of Chloe's dad. Tall, dark and handsome sounded such a cliché, but suited her little student's father to a tee. The touch of Saturday stubble and the faint scar that decorated his cheek added, rather than detracted from his overall appeal.

Annabel swallowed. This was Chloe's father. Chloe's mother's husband or partner, for goodness' sake. *Not available.*

She forced her face into a polite smile.

"Hi, Teacher." His voice was deep.

Not available.

"Oh, call me Annabel." For the first time, she regretted Coombethwaite School's policy of introducing themselves by their first names to parents.

"In that case, you must call me Daniel." Blue eyes exactly the same shade as his little daughter's looked into hers. His mouth curved into a lazy smile. "I'm glad to meet the teacher that Chloe hasn't stopped talking about since term started."

Was it hot in here? Annabel crushed the urge to fan herself. Really, his wife shouldn't let him out on his own. Predatory women were everywhere—and there were plenty who wouldn't think twice about responding to the hint of flirtation in his expression. Annabel knew all about them from bitter experience.

No-one would ever accuse her of flirting with some other woman's man.

"I'm going to get my hair cut!" Chloe said, "I was telling Daddy…"

"She wants her hair cut just like yours." Daniel lifted one of Chloe's plaits. "She's been trying to explain your haircut to me all morning." The glance he shot at his daughter was full of warmth.

"Just ask for a bob with a fringe."

Unlike lots of the children in her class, Chloe wasn't picked up by either parent at the end of the school day, but instead by an older woman who Chloe had explained was her granny. Presumably her mum was busy this morning too.

"Thanks." That smile again.

Annabel crossed her legs.

Daniel rubbed the side of his head. "I was worried it would make her look too grown up. I like…"

"Daddy likes my hair in plaits. But every morning when Daddy brushes my hair for school it takes ages, and then I have to wait while he plaits it." Chloe frowned.

"I think a bob will look lovely on you, Chloe."

Daniel glanced at his watch. "I better grab my coffee and get out of here if we're going to make our appointment." He extended a large tanned hand.

She put her hand into his, feeling warmth tingle from the point of contact as his fingers curved around hers. Under his gaze, the detached distance she'd sought shifted.

"Good to meet you."

Words dried in her throat. She should say something. Instead, she pulled her hand away and rubbed it on her jeans out of sight under the table, in a vague attempt to stop the tingling his touch had started.

Daniel looked down at the table. His smile widened. "Are you enjoying it?"

For a mad moment, Annabel wondered if he was referring to the electricity sparking between them. She blinked, then followed his gaze.

Her paperback. The latest novel from her favourite crime writer. The writer that her ex-boyfriend had constantly mocked, to her eternal irritation.

And now, another man was grinning at her choice of reading material.

She sat up straighter on the chair. "It's wonderful. He's a great writer."

If there was a hint of chill in her voice, a hint of challenge in the eyes that she focused in his direction, so be it. No-one got to dictate to her what she should or shouldn't read, or anything else for that matter. Especially if they couldn't even…

The look on Daniel Walker's face was difficult to decipher. If she had to put a name to it, she'd have said it combined shock and confusion.

"See you on Monday, Teacher!" Chloe tugged on Daniel's hand.

"Bye." With the hint of a wry smile, he let himself be led away.

Chapter Two

As he was the only retained firefighter with a child in Coombethwaite Primary at the moment, Daniel volunteered to do the annual 'fire-safety' talk. It meant a morning away from the computer, but he wasn't getting many words down on paper this week anyway. Not since the chance meeting with Chloe's teacher on Saturday.

Annabel. Her name danced in his head. Every day since the beginning of term he'd been regaled with stories about her. His little daughter had a serious fixation on her teacher, and he couldn't blame her. Teacher was gorgeous.

She hadn't stood, but she was obviously tall, if those long legs were any indication. And her blonde hair cut into a bob had been mussed, as though she'd just clambered out of bed—a look that Chloe's mother would never have gone for.

He pulled on his fire jacket, and reached for his fire-axe. No, Melanie was more of a 'polished at all times' woman. A woman who had everything totally under control. A well-ordered life plan that never included becoming pregnant.

Daniel's fingers tightened on the axe. At least she'd had the decency to carry their baby to term. And hadn't stood in the way of his bid for full custody. He hadn't heard anything from her since shortly after she gave birth to their daughter. She'd breast fed Chloe for two days, two days where he felt sure she'd change her mind about being a mother—who could resist the adorable baby she held in her arms? So even when she'd packed her belongings in the hospital, accepted a cheque to tide her over until she was able to continue her high powered job in the city, part of Daniel had hoped…

He rubbed his jaw, the stubble rough beneath his fingers.

There was no point going back over the past. Melanie hadn't wanted to be a mother. *Ever*. And even her beautiful daughter hadn't been able to jump start her maternal instinct. In the six years since, they hadn't heard anything from her.

He couldn't imagine a moment when he hadn't wanted a child. And the moment Chloe came into the world was the moment his world became complete. Unfortunately the same couldn't be said for his daughter. She was part of a warm, strong family. With a granny who took up the slack, picking her up from school every day, while he wrote. She had more aunties and cousins than most of her classmates, all of them local and a very real part of her life. But still, she hadn't got a mummy. The lack of one was becoming an issue.

He snagged his fire helmet, and strode to his car. She was so excited about him talking in school today; she'd barely been able to stand still as he brushed her hair that morning. She'd even wanted him to arrive in the fire engine, saying Teacher would love that.

At the thought of Annabel Jackson, warmth pooled in Daniel's stomach. His mother Janice had been diligent in passing on the fact that her granddaughter's teacher was single. In fact, he almost suspected Janice and Chloe of plotting a match.

Unfortunately romance with his daughter's teacher wasn't an option. There'd been women since Chloe's birth, but none of them had met his daughter—there was no way he'd put Chloe through the heartbreak when they left.

Chapter Three

The headmistress had a thing for firefighters. *Who knew?*

Although if truth be told, every woman on the planet probably had a thing for wide-shouldered men with hero complexes. The fact that Olga Blakeney was a respectably married woman didn't seem to affect her enthusiasm at the prospect of this morning's visit from Daniel Walker. She was a woman aflutter.

"He's such an interesting man," she confided to Annabel in the staff-room during their mid-morning break. "So talented too."

Annabel reached for a chocolate chip cookie.

"He's a writer, you know. And so dedicated to his daughter." Olga smoothed back her greying hair with ink-stained fingers. She sipped her tea. "Being a single father must be very difficult."

"I didn't know…"

Olga leaned close. "He's brought Chloe up totally alone. Of course, his mother is a wonderful woman. I was in school with Janice you know. When that woman…" Olga's lips pursed as though she'd sucked on a lemon. "Well, I shouldn't really talk about their family's private business."

"Of course." Annabel wanted to know more. He was a writer? The fact that he'd grinned at her choice of reading material stung even more with that revelation. The news that he was a single dad was welcome—despite her best efforts, she hadn't been able to banish the inappropriate thoughts that had snuck up on her when she wasn't guarding against them. There had been heat in their brief encounter, heat she hadn't been able to deny, or to deal with. The fact that he wasn't a shameless cheater was a huge relief.

"Should we bring all the children in to the assembly room straight after break?"

Olga nodded. "Yes, we should set up before he arrives." Her eyes took on a glazed look. "I hope he comes in full firefighter gear."

Annabel schooled her features into a neutral expression. With an entire school's complement of female teachers, there would be quite enough hero worship to go around; there was no need to add herself to the collection of firefighter groupies. Although she did secretly find the idea of Daniel dressed as her private fantasy, pretty well…hot.

Fifteen minutes later, all ninety children were seated on the floor of the assembly room. The buzz of childish conversation, after much shushing, was slightly quieter than usual.

The door cracked open, and the headmistress walked in, casting her gaze back and forth, wordlessly demanding silence. Daniel walked behind her, in full firefighter kit—his helmet on, and his fire axe held across his powerful chest.

"OMG, be still my beating heart," whispered Susie, teacher of Year Two.

Oh, mine too. When Daniel reached the front of the room, he took off his helmet and placed it on the desk, shaking his head slightly, like in a shampoo commercial.

The children cheered.

Annabel couldn't blame them, she felt like cheering herself.

He turned to the teachers. "Good morning, ladies."

Wow, was Olga actually *blushing?*

He smiled at their mumbled responses, making brief eye contact with Annabel.

She smiled back, feeling her face warm with a flush. Which

was totally ridiculous. Before she had time to analyse her response, he turned to the roomful of children.

"Good morning, children." He reserved a special smile and nod for his daughter, who beamed with pride. "Today we're going to talk about all the things you can do to make sure that your house is safe."

Annabel's heart clenched at the sight of all the rapt faces taking in his every word. As he spoke about making sure that everyone in their family knew what to do in case of a fire, carefully stressing the need to have an emergency plan, her heart melted into a puddle.

The allocated half hour of fire safety talk flew by, and before she knew it, they were handing out the fire-safety notes he'd brought with him, including badges for the children depicting cartoon firefighters.

"I think we should show our appreciation for Chloe's dad's visit today, children," Olga said, giving her approval for the enthusiastic clapping that followed. "Now, get into your lines, and it's back to class." She turned to Annabel. "I'll see your class back to the classroom. Could you see Mr Walker out?" *Was there a twinkle in her eyes?*

"Of course." Annabel reached for the axe as Daniel picked up his helmet.

The sky was dark with threatened rain as she pushed the door open. "The children really enjoyed that."

"I did too."

They strode to his car, and she waited as he stripped off his bulky jacket and tossed it on the back seat. As he reached for the axe, their hands touched. Neither moved.

His hand was warm atop hers. His gaze held her captive.

Electricity seemed to hum in the air, sparking as his gaze fell to her parted lips.

"Would you like to go to dinner with me, sometime?" The words were spoken quickly, as if he hadn't considered them, but was acting on impulse.

"I…" Dating a student's father was…well, was there anything wrong with it?

"We could talk about your choice of reading material." His mouth curved into a grin.

Another superior male who considered her reading tastes trashy? Annabel felt her mouth compress, as her hazy, romantic mood shattered. "What have you got against WD Daniels, anyway?" The harshness of her words was punctuated with her shoving the axe into his chest.

Daniel's eyes widened. "Nothing!" He rubbed the back of his neck as realisation dawned. "God, you don't know, do you?"

Crossing her arms felt satisfying. As if she was conveying 'hands off' without even having to say it. "What?"

"I love the fact that you read my books." He grinned, after a stunned moment of silence. "Watch out, you'll catch flies."

She closed her mouth. Shook her head. "You're WD Daniels?"

Daniel reached for her hand. "The very same. Want to have dinner tomorrow night, and find out about Harper's newest adventure?"

Chapter Four

Daniel picked her up promptly the following evening. He wore plain black trousers, and a black shirt open at the neck, and topped it off with a thick sheepskin jacket. *Snugglicious*. His hair was brushed back. "I thought we'd go over the hill to Morton and have dinner there at a little Italian restaurant I know."

Annabel reached for her coat and handbag, ready on the side table next to the door.

"Let me help you." Daniel took the coat from her hands and held it open.

She turned her back, sliding an arm into the wool coat's slippery silken lining. Felt the brush of his fingers as he flicked her hair from the collar in a gesture that was innocent yet strangely personal. A shiver chased up her spine. The electricity between them was impossible to ignore. "You found a babysitter okay?" She locked the door behind them, and followed him to his car.

"My sister has taken Chloe for the night. The cousins jump at any chance for a sleepover, and it's easier than pulling my sister out of her house to babysit in mine." He opened the car door with a smile.

So there'd be no need to hurry back. Annabel linked her hands on the lap of her scarlet dress, feeling the floaty layers of material slide against the stiffer lining. She'd worried about meeting up with other parents or teachers in the couple of places to eat in Coombethwaite. The fact he'd chosen a restaurant further away meant they would be less likely to bump into people they knew.

"I've signed off duty for the fire service too." His mouth curved into a grin as he cast a glance her direction in the darkened car interior. "There's nothing worse than getting dragged out in the middle of a meal."

The car crested the top of the hill and below, the lights of Morton shone in the darkness. Before long, they'd driven into the centre of the village, found a parking spot, and hurried into the warm restaurant.

In mere moments, they were seated at an intimate table in the corner. A candle in a clear glass candlestick set the scene, and a small posy of red roses and carnations looked pretty in the flickering light. The waiter brought them menus, and left them alone.

"This is lovely." Shyness tied Annabel's tongue, now that the date was actually happening. It had been months since she'd been out with a man alone. Before she left London, a few friends had dragged her out with them in the hope of introducing her to a new man—she'd refused the blind dates they'd tried to set her up with. Being alone was better, way easier than jumping into the dating pool. Because when it came down to it, men couldn't be trusted, not with her heart. She'd given it once to someone she thought she loved. His betrayal had shaken her belief in her own ability to weed the good guys from the bad.

"You're frowning." Daniel spoke quietly. "Is there a problem?"

Annabel tried a smile, but it felt false. "I was just thinking of something." She concentrated on the menu. "Everything looks good. I'm going to have trouble choosing!"

Earnest blue eyes gazed into hers. "You can tell me, you know." He wasn't talking about food. "We can be friends."

Friends were the one thing missing from her new life. She had a great job, somewhere nice to live, but hadn't really found a friend. If friendship was the only thing Daniel wanted…

"I'd like us to be more." His hand covered hers.

Annabel swallowed. "I've had my heart broken." The words sounded bleak. She hadn't wanted to reveal so much, so soon.

"Tell me." His hand squeezed hers.

"I'm sure we can think of something else to talk about rather than my sad story."

The waiter started across the room, notepad at the ready.

On the point of answering, Daniel spotted the waiter's approach. He released her hand. "Let's order."

She'd been rude. Once they'd ordered and were alone again, Annabel regretted her response. "I'm sorry, I…"

"I understand. I've been there." He pushed a hand through his hair. "Chloe's mum didn't want to be pregnant. She stayed long enough to have the baby, then left Chloe with me."

Annabel's heart clenched. *How could any woman abandon her baby?* "She…"

"She hasn't been back." Daniel reached for a breadstick, and snapped it. "Chloe is better off without her, and I love her enough for both parents." His jaw was tight. "My family are great; they've given Chloe the extended family that she needs. Others to love her as well as her father."

Annabel breathed deeply. "I was engaged. My fiancé Steven slept with my best friend two weeks before the wedding. He'd probably been sleeping with her for a while—I didn't wait around to find out."

Daniel's eyes closed. His face contorted in a wince. "God, that must have hurt."

Lingering pain burned in Annabel's chest. She'd been such a blind fool. "It did. I guess I wanted the happy ever after so badly I blocked all the signs. He was a salesman, and was always away on trips. Looking back, I should have suspected…"

Daniel's eyes opened. "Why should you? You thought he was honest. Don't blame yourself because you weren't suspicious. How long ago did this happen?"

"Six months. I switched schools and moved to Coombethwaite for a new start." Her once-upon-a-time friend's daughter went to Annabel's previous school. The prospect of facing Steven at the school gates had been much too painful to contemplate.

Daniel raised his glass and clinked it against hers. "Let's drink to that."

"I got defensive in the café when we first met, because I thought you were criticising my favourite author." Annabel grinned. "Steven wasn't a fan."

"No loss, by the sound of him." Daniel grinned back. "So, I'm your favourite author?" There was warmth in his eyes.

"Well, Harper is my favourite character." She gave in to an unexpected urge to flirt, leaning in close and fluttering her eyelashes. "I don't suppose he's based on a real guy? Someone who works in the fire station, maybe?"

"I guess you'd like an introduction?"

"You guess right."

Daniel laughed. "I can't imagine a loner like Harper settling in Coombethwaite, can you?" His gaze fell to her lips, and suddenly the humour evaporated, replaced by a heat that seared. "Luckily, as his creator, I guess I'm the next best thing."

Silence hung in the air between them for a long moment.

"I guess you are." Her voice sounded husky.

Daniel lifted her hand to his lips and kissed her knuckles.

The breath left Annabel's lungs, and instantly all she could think of was his mouth trailing slowly down her neck. Heat pooled in her stomach.

A cleared throat. "Your meal…" The waiter stood by the table, balancing two plates aloft.

Without a trace of embarrassment, Daniel released her hand. "Let's eat."

Chapter Five

Every moment of the evening was pure magic. The attraction that had smouldered inside since Chloe's introduction in the café, sparked to life with every glance from Annabel's green eyes. Daniel didn't want forever, but didn't know how to damp down the feelings she brought to life in him as they talked through the night. Maybe it was crazy even to try.

The fact she didn't know she was gorgeous turned him on. And the way she responded to his touch, the way her eyes darkened when he asked if she was ready to leave... well it hinted that he wasn't the only one feeling the heat.

She's Chloe's teacher. If things go wrong...

Resistance was completely futile. He could no more say no to her than he could resist breathing. He reached for her hand as they walked out into the dark night across the car park to his car.

"I enjoyed this evening." Annabelle's breath puffed out in little clouds in the frigid air. She stopped as he pressed the tab to unlock the car, and turned.

His arms came around her in a predestined move, and without hesitation, she stepped close, resting her hands on his chest as her face tilted to his.

Her lips parted the moment his touched, allowing him access, and when their tongues tangled she pulled him closer on a moan. Her soft breasts encased in the red dress that had ignited lust the moment he'd seen her at her front door, pressed against his chest. His hands skimmed her back, sliding over her bottom as he brought the rest of her body in line with his.

He was always in control, always.

Not now. The urge to have her in his bed, stripped of the filmy red fabric, blazed.

Daniel cracked open an eye to see a sliver of light as a car circled. He pulled his mouth from hers as it accelerated quickly past them. He caught a brief glance of the car's occupant. A woman. Driving much too fast in the icy conditions.

Annabel touched her mouth, and shivered. "We should…"

Daniel nodded. "Let's go. It's freezing." He pressed his mouth to hers in a brief kiss, then opened the door for her.

Black ice made the road treacherous, but at least there was no traffic on the route home. Daniel turned up the heater. On a night like this one five years ago he'd lost his friend John on this very road. Black ice demanded all of his attention.

"Your place or mine?" Annabel asked.

He couldn't risk taking his eyes off the road for a moment, but the quiet question reignited in an instant the erection he'd been concentrating on controlling.

"Oh, I'm sorry, that sounded so cheesy…" Annabel sounded embarrassed.

"It sounded great. Let's go to mine." He stared through the windscreen, smearing now with traces of the fog that fell so suddenly here, close to the hill's summit. "The road is treacherous tonight, otherwise I'd…"

Ahead, tail lights shone watery red at an angle from the road. An angle that indicated the car was in the ditch, or worse.

"Damn!" Daniel braked slowly, feeling the car start to slide on the invisible black ice, before righting itself. He pulled over behind the car and turned the hazard lights on. "There's a blanket in the back, could you get it for me?" He glanced at Annabel's white face. "Bring your phone."

She nodded, and pulled on her coat.

Quickly, Daniel made his way to the car. He checked for

smoke or flames, and breathed easier when he didn't find any. The front passenger side had collided with a tree, and glancing inside, he saw the driver's airbag hadn't deployed. The crash hadn't been at excessive speed, at any rate. "Are you okay? Can you move?" The back seats were empty, and he recognised the woman from the restaurant car park.

She didn't move, but her eyes were open. "Miss?

Wincing, she turned.

Daniel opened the door, turned off the engine, slipped the keys into his pocket, and left the car lights on. "Can you move?"

"I...I think so." Her fingers curved into her thighs as she moved her feet up and down. "Yes, I....ow."

"Steady." It was to be expected she'd have a bruise, maybe even a cracked rib if she'd been jerked hard against the seat-belt. "Any other pain apart from across here?" His fingers traced the path of the seat-belt across her body.

"My chest hurts."

"What's your name?" It was an important detail to find out in case she went unconscious. Someone, somewhere, would be worried about her when she didn't make it home.

"Felicity Markham." Her eyes closed.

"Stay with me, Felicity."

"I have the blanket."

Daniel turned at the sound of Annabel's voice.

"Call the ambulance." Quickly and efficiently he reeled off the car's location and gave her rough details to pass on.

"Let's see if we can get you out."

Felicity's eyes flickered open. She was going into shock, but the ambulance would be with them in a matter of moments. The car seemed safe enough, but there was always the possibility of a collision if another car lost control on the slippery surface. He needed to get her out of the car.

The seat-belt unfastened easily, and with help, she stepped out the car.

"Could you lay the blanket down on the grass?" With a jerk of his head, Daniel showed Annabel a spot on the verge, away from danger if any other car suffered the same fate as hers had on this treacherous night. Annabel ran ahead, and did as he asked.

"I found a silver blanket in the back too."

Daniel nodded. He always kept emergency supplies in his car. In winter, having an emergency space-blanket could be the difference between life and death if caught in a snowstorm. "That's great." He carefully helped Felicity to sit, then shrouded the light foil over her shoulders.

She was shivering. Daniel pulled off his sheepskin coat and draped it over the space-blanket. "The ambulance will be here soon." He held her hand, offering comfort, as the faint sound of a siren grew stronger, heralding the imminent arrival of an ambulance.

Chapter Six

Annabel stood on the grass verge in the darkness and watched Daniel talk to the ambulance crew. He pulled the car keys from his pocket, speaking all the time, passing on vital information. In his role as firefighter, he obviously knew the ambulance crew well. By the time they had Felicity safely inside, Annabel's fingers were cramped with cold. She flexed them, picked up the blankets and Daniel's coat from the frost-crisped grass, and walked to the car.

Through the windscreen, she saw the ambulance driver thump Daniel on the back—man shorthand for acknowledging a job well done. Daniel was still smiling as he walked to the car.

"She'll be fine." He turned on the engine, and dialled the heat up full. "I better get you home."

"Wait." She needed to tell him, needed to show him. Annabel reached for the side of Daniel's face, trailing her fingers across the slash of his cheekbone to the back of his head. Pulling him in for her kiss. Without even trying, just by being himself, so warm and caring to a stranger in peril on the road, he'd shown the sort of man he was. The sort of man who gave. The sort of man who cared. The sort of man that she could give her heart to, without fear.

His lips moved over hers in a caress that heated far more efficiently than the warm air blowing at her frigid feet. His hands cupped either side of her head, holding her in place, thumbs slowly stroking her jawline.

By the time he pulled away, her heart was pounding like a jackhammer. Denim eyes stared into hers.

"Let's go home."

Annabel traced her top lip with her tongue, feeling the shadow imprint of his mouth. One word encapsulated every emotion tumbling inside perfectly. "Yes."

The journey through the inky blackness felt predestined. Like the planets high overhead were perfectly aligned. Every step up Daniel's path to the front door was a step away from the heartache of the past, towards a new future, one glittering with possibilities.

There was no need for words. No pretence of making coffee. As the door closed behind Annabel, Daniel turned her into his arms and pressed his mouth insistently to hers. The door was hard against her back as Daniel stripped off her coat and her fingers simultaneously slipped his heavy sheepskin jacket from his shoulders.

His hands gripped her hips, pulling her so close the hard evidence of his arousal pressed against her stomach. In a haze of sensation, Annabel rose up on tiptoe, wanting, needing more.

Without breaking the perfect melding of their mouths, Daniel lifted her.

Annabel's legs hooked around his back as he held her secure with one hand under her bottom, and climbed the stairs.

In the bedroom, he slowly let her down. The glow of the streetlight outside the window slanted through a gap in the curtains, illuminating the room with a soft, magical light. Without words, he unzipped her dress and slid it from her shoulders.

"You're beautiful." His voice was deep.

Standing in her underwear, Annabel was glad she'd decided against tights and worn stockings instead. She stared at his chest, shaking fingers undoing every button on his black shirt.

His chest... There was a reason why women had fantasies about firefighters. Daniel's upper chest was perfect. Wide, with powerful muscles perfectly defined. Her fingers trailed down his stomach, feeling each curve and dip beneath her fingertips. When she reached the top button of his trousers, he moved quickly, pulling her close and joining their mouths again.

The next few frantic moments flew by and then she was on the bed, naked, with an equally naked Daniel cupping her breasts with his powerful hands. Hands that could be gentle, could be caring, just like the man.

"You have a freckle on your breast." Daniel traced it with his tongue. "It's sexy."

Laughter bubbled up, and Annabel let it free. "You have an awesome body, but you know that, right?"

Daniel looked up.

She shivered at the touch of his chin on her bare skin.

"No-one's ever told me that before." He grinned.

Annabel tapped her lips with her index finger. "Come up here," she whispered. "And I'll tell you what I'd like you to do with it."

Daniel shook his head. "I have a plan. You'll like it."

And as he kissed his way down her body, Annabel had to agree that she did.

Chapter Seven

After a morning spent staring at his computer screen, checking email, reading blogs, and basically doing everything except what he should be doing, Daniel flicked off his monitor and strode into the kitchen.

The past month had passed so quickly he couldn't believe it. Already, his mother had started to ask what he and Chloe were doing for Christmas. They'd alternated between his mother and sister for the holiday since Chloe was born—Chloe loved the buzz of family at Christmastime.

But a Christmas wouldn't include Annabel. Not unless he changed things. Made her publicly a part of not only his life, but Chloe's.

He threw out the old grounds from the coffee machine, and mechanically started a new batch. A couple of nights a week, he sent Chloe to stay with her granny to give him and Annabel some time together. It felt like sneaking around. And he was sick to death of it.

This morning, Chloe'd asked if Teacher was his girlfriend. Her eyes had lit with unmasked hope. Hope that Teacher might become Mummy. He'd done what he'd always swore he'd never do, and told his beloved daughter that they'd talk about it later.

He sat at the kitchen counter. Gazed at the pictures stuck on the fridge. Right now, Annabel and Chloe were together, as they were every day. In the role of teacher and pupil. And Annabel wanted to keep up the pretence that they were nothing more than that, fearful that dating her student's father would somehow affect her standing in the tiny school.

Coombethwaite was curtain-twitch central. The gossip had started already. The guys at the firestation were always asking him to bring Annabel out to the pub, to introduce her, but the snatched moments they had together were too fleeting, too important to share.

He poured a cup of coffee, adding a splash of cold water from the tap.

Last night, she'd stayed over. Laid out her small collection of toiletries on the edge of the sink. They'd made love long into the night, her scent clung to his sheets even after every other trace of her had been tidied away into the bag that she stowed in her boot. Just like always.

Like a man in a dream, Daniel clutched the coffee cup and trudged up the stairs. There was a dent in her pillow. A discarded earring lay on the carpet half under the bed.

Daniel stooped and picked it up. Placed it carefully on the bedside table, where he wanted it to be. He'd wanted everything once, and for a blind minute had thought the woman he was with wanted it too. How long was he going to let the lessons of the past dictate his future?

He'd never believed he could fall in love so quickly, so totally. This Christmas, he wanted Annabel's clothes in his wardrobe. His ring on her finger. His daughter to have a mother. And more than a lover, he wanted Annabel as his wife. Forever.

He glanced at the alarm clock. Twelve o'clock. The parent/teacher meeting was at three. He had time.

#

Annabel had a hidden agenda, and she wasn't ashamed to admit it to herself. She'd scheduled Daniel as the last parent of the day, purely so she could stretch out the allocated ten minutes to fifteen. Five extra minutes they could spend together without igniting gossip.

She shook Teddy McDonald's parents' hands and assured them he would get over throwing all the dolls out of the playhouse—it was just that with a firefighter as an uncle he wanted to play fireman all the time. And that she'd talked to him about it. Told him that the girls found it upsetting. They'd come up with a solution, a compromise. He could play fire on Fridays, the rest of the week the girls played house.

As the grateful parents left, Annabel nipped out to the watercooler in the corridor. Olga was already there, filling a small plastic cup.

"Only one more to go for me, how about you?" Olga asked.

"Just one more, yes." Annabel glanced down the stairs. No sign of Daniel, but then she'd finished early, and he wasn't expected for another few minutes.

"Daniel Walker?" Olga's eyebrows rose.

Annabel nodded.

"Chloe is a lovely child."

Annabel's heart swelled. "Yes." She wanted to say so much more. How every day the sight of Annabel's little face as she came into the classroom filled her with joy. Her eyes matched Daniel's, how could she fail to love the little girl as if she was her own? Daniel wanted to keep the lines clearly drawn. He'd explained early on that Chloe was the most important person in his life. That he didn't date because he didn't want Chloe to become close to a woman who might not stick around forever.

"We all know you're dating Daniel, you know." Olga sipped her water, her gaze piercing. She leaned in and spoke quietly. "And we approve. He's a lovely man who deserves some happiness."

Annabel breathed in. Apparently her attempts to keep their romance under wraps had been woefully inadequate. "I thought…well…me being Chloe's teacher…" Word failed her.

"You thought that the other parents would judge you? Or the teachers would?" Olga's eyebrow arched. "You're not exactly the femme fatale type." She softened her words with a smile. "No-one has a problem with it. Love—"

Footsteps on the stairs. Heavy ones.

Annabel peeked over the bannisters.

"Ah, here's my last appointment."

Olga winked. Refilled her cup, and strode into her classroom, closing the door quietly.

"Hi." Daniel was wearing his thick sheepskin jacket.

Annabel clenched the plastic cup tight to resist throwing her arms around him. She always wanted to. But this wasn't the place.

She stepped back, opened her classroom door wide and followed him to the desk.

He perched on the tiny chair made for six year olds, with his hands resting on his knees.

"You tell me every day about Chloe's progress." Daniel stared into her eyes. "But I guess I had to come in."

Annabel swiped her top lip with her tongue. "Every parent has to come to the parent/teacher meetings. It's awkward this year…" she looked at the page in front of her on the desk. "Because you and I are dating, but next year it'll be different, she'll have another teacher."

Daniel smiled that smile that made her heart flip. "Next year you'll be at the meeting too, though won't you?"

Confusion swirled within. "There won't be any need for it. Chloe's doing really well at school. She's happy, well adjusted, and a very good student." She shuffled the papers. "You have nothing to worry about."

Daniel stood and shoved his hand into his pocket. "I have got something to worry about." The look in his eyes turned her insides to water.

"I don't want to play this game any more."

Breathing became difficult. In such a short amount of time, Daniel and Chloe had become her entire world. She couldn't imagine a life without him in it, but apparently he didn't feel the same. Pain pierced her heart. She clamped her eyes tight shut.

"Annabel."

When she opened them, he wasn't where she expected him to be, but instead on one knee before her, clutching a small blue velvet box.

"Will you come to the parent/teacher meeting with me next year, as my wife?"

"God, yes." She launched herself from the chair into his arms, kissing him with a joy that knew no limits.

Daniel's phone beeped. Annabel pulled away, perching on the edge of the chair as he opened the box and slipped a beautiful opal ring on her finger. His phone beeped again.

"You better get that, it might be urgent."

Daniel stood and fished the phone from his pocket. Then he sighed.

"What?"

"I popped in to my mother's on the way here to talk to Chloe. I asked her permission to propose." He ran a hand through his hair, then pulled Annabel into his arms. "She was so excited, and it appears the secret's out." He waved the phone. "She's brought my mother to the school, and outside that door, is the whole Walker posse wanting to know your answer."

"Well in that case…" Annabel's fingers ran through Daniel's hair, bringing him close for her kiss. "Hurry up and kiss me."

About the author:

Sally Clements writes fun, sexy and real contemporary romance, partnering hot heroes with heroines that know what they want, and go for it! Always a voracious reader, she considers writing for a living the perfect job—the only downside is saying goodbye to her characters at book's end.

She's @sallywriter on twitter.
And she's on facebook

Sally's Books

Catch Me A Catch
Bound to Love
Marrying Cade
Challenging Andie
Angel All Year
Runaway Groom
Love on the Vine
The Morning After
New Beginnings (short stories)

Worth the Risk

Tara Pammi

Chapter One

"Have you lost your mind?"

The words rumbled across the small room towards Annie Bennett. She shivered even as every inch of her grew hot from the small fire in the room. The moment the fire had started getting out of hand, she'd started praying fervently. Not that the fire would subside, but that it wouldn't be Marcus who got called.

No dice.

A bucket of water greeted her next, drenching her from head to toe, putting out the last lick of fire that was scorching through her old recliner. She clenched her fingers on the blanket in her hand. She coughed, trying to breathe past the coils of smoke.

Strong hands gripped her waist and hauled her upright. Annie's heart began a tattoo. Dear God, she would know that touch in a coma. Huge palms patted down her back, an arm still thrown about her middle.

He turned her around roughly.

"You should know better than to…." Callused fingers pushed her chin up. A tremor started in the base of her spine the same second she heard his sharp hiss of breath.

The tension curling around them had nothing on the smoke. "Annie?"

Annie nodded and blinked. His blue gaze drilling into her, Marcus looked like he had seen a ghost. She had no such problems. She hungrily stared at him, taking in the strong jaw, the jet black hair combed back from a high forehead.

"When the hell did you get into town?"

His hard voice interrupting her greedy perusal, she stepped back from him. Mrs. Z, standing at the entrance to her room, had a totally righteous expression on her face.

"A week ago." A scratching began in her throat, and she coughed. Her own body was in revolt, apparently. "And the fire wasn't that bad. I almost had it covered."

"God, Annie. You show up after three years and like this?"

She shrugged. And wiped her trembling hand over her forehead. She had no answer for his unasked question, not one that would satisfy him anyway.

Words weren't going to come, not past the tears gathering in her throat. His frown still in place, Marcus enfolded her in his arms. He smelled of smoke like she did, but beneath that, she could breathe the scent of him, feel the familiar warmth from his body seeping into hers. Emotions and memories exploded within her, but just as quickly he thrust her back from him.

As though he regretted the hug.

"What have you been burning?" he said, his tone under perfect control, his gaze taking in the cardboard box on the coffee table in the middle of the room, and the charred remains of her sofa bed. But she had seen the hurt flash in his eyes.

She forced herself to meet his gaze. "Photos and cards from my ex."

He scowled, even the soot on his face not diluting its intensity. "Who even has hard copies anymore?" He rolled his eyes at her continuing silence. "Wait a second. You ordered copies so you could burn them, didn't you?"

This time, she couldn't stop the smile pulling at her mouth. See, even after five years, no one in London understood her as Marcus did. "It's a ritual, Marcus."

"Why here?" A simple question, loaded with anger and so much more. "Couldn't it wait till you're back in London?"

Her little ritual had forced this confrontation far sooner than she had expected. But that was one of her goals. Wasn't it?

To take risks, to grab happiness where she could. She swallowed and forced a casualness she was far from feeling into her words. "For one thing, it has to be done on the night of New Year's Eve. Secondly," her breath almost choked her, "I'm back in Coombethwaite, Marcus. For good."

#

Standing outside the cottage, Marcus looked up at the perfect sky.

Annie was back. And *for good* apparently, whatever the hell that meant.

His chest tightened, and he exhaled on a long rush. With a lighter heart, he dialed the chief's number and gave him a quick report, leaving Annie's name out of it. It wouldn't even be an official report because Mrs. Z had called him when she had started smelling the smoke.

And she had picked *him* because it was Annie.

He didn't want to feel the lightness spreading inside him, couldn't stem the soft joy gushing through him.

But, damn it, he had missed her. He had needed her but she hadn't been there. Funny thing was he had missed her even before Grace had died. And having known her- hell, he'd met Grace through Annie, Grace had understood that. His wonderful wife had understood that as much as he loved her, he'd missed his best friend when she had all but disappeared from their lives.

"I'm ready," she whispered behind him. He turned. She had thrown a jacket on without changing her wet clothes. Her delicate face was all angles in the faint moonlight, the stubborn angle of her jaw set tight. Soft snow was beginning to fall, and a flake landed on her nose.

Dark blue shadows danced under her eyes and she looked tired. He felt that same squeeze in his chest again.

She wore her dark brown hair long again, though those bangs, forever hanging into her eyes, hid her expression from him. She hitched her backpack over her shoulder. "Although I really don't think there's any need."

He glared at her. "That room is filled with smoke, Annie. Unless you prefer that Mr. Z call the whole town. Any number of people will offer to take you in then."

That had her pick up her pace from the porch and head towards his cottage.

They walked in silence for a while. And it was exactly as he had remembered between them.

He was still angry that she had cut herself out of his life without explanation. But the silence between them had that warm, comfortable quality to it that brought a smile to his face. Simply enough, silence shared with Annie made him less lonely than a crowd full of well-meaning friends.

Catching up to her, he grabbed her hair as he had done so many times when they were growing up. She squealed when he pulled her to his side.

Sparks flew from her brown gaze. "Not funny, Marcus."

He loosened his grip but didn't let go. Damn, but she felt good against him. All warm, cuddly and still a little sooty. He grinned just like that. "So what did this poor guy do?"

She stiffened under his hold. "Fell in love with a friend of mine."

"Ouch," he said, feigning mock pity.

She decked him in his ribs with a surprise move, her mouth set tight. "It isn't funny, Marcus. *It hurts.*" A curse flew from her mouth, dealing an invisible punch. "I'm sick and tired of people thinking Annie doesn't mind, Annie doesn't have feelings."

He stared at her and felt a strange tightness in his gut, a sneaking feeling that there was something he wasn't seeing. "God, Annie. I never thought that."

"Didn't you, Marcus?" She picked up her backpack from the ground and shied her gaze away from him. "It's my own damn fault anyway. All my life, I've played the good friend, the good daughter, even the good arrellin. I even went to bloody London because it was my dad's last wish."

"Yes, because he wanted you to see other places," he said, unable to resist pointing the obvious. "The decision to stay there for four years was yours."

"And what was I supposed to come back…" She hesitated, and turned away from him. "It's going to change from today."

He braced himself. "What do you mean?"

"I'm going to grab life by the horns, Marcus," she said, with a funny little glance his way. "I'm going to be selfish. I'm going to do what I want."

Chapter Two

They reached Marcus's lakeside cottage a few minutes short of midnight. Annie could hear the hoots and laughter from the village square just as she climbed the steps to the main door. "Aren't you going?" she said almost hopefully.

He pushed open the door to his cottage and hovered at the entrance. "No. You?"

"God, no," she said, a shiver flaring over her skin. "That's all I need-"

His hand on her wrist tugged her back. "Afraid everyone will tell you how much they have missed you?"

It was the displeasure in his words more than the content that stopped Annie short. Just as the first chime reverberated all over the tiny village.

"Just because I lived in London doesn't mean I don't care about anyone here."

The silence around them was heavy with unspoken words. Another chime. Fourth or fifth, Annie lost count.

Suddenly an idea sprang into her mind, her insides vibrating at the mere thought.

She gazed at him, studying the hard planes of his face. "Did you, Marcus?"

He frowned. "Did I what?"

Number nine.

"Miss me?"

"Do you care?"

Number ten.

This was it. She would never have the courage to ask Marcus to kiss her otherwise. This way, she at least had an excuse. Wasn't this what her ritual had been about?

Goodbye to old pain, and welcome to new risks.

She moved down from the steps, and the eleventh chime struck.

She cupped his jaw as she had done so many times. And yet he already felt different to her. "I missed you, Marcus, a lot. I wanted to come and see you so many times."

"Hell, Annie. Why didn't you? You left Grace's funeral before I could even get a chance to talk to you."

"It was for the best."

His gaze searched hers as though he was seeing her anew. As though he had suddenly realized that there was more to her.

Hell, yeah, there was.

Twelfth chime struck and hoots and yells could be heard from the square. Fireworks blazed in the sky.

Annie dropped her hands on his shoulder, bent her torso forward. Her breath stuck somewhere between her chest and her throat. "Happy New Year, Marcus," she whispered, bending low, and pressed her mouth to his.

#

She tasted like soot and coal. He knew this because he was kissing *Annie*.

The thought spun around in infinite little circles in Marcus's head.

He was kissing the girl whose pigtails had driven him to do crazy things. He was kissing the girl who had sat through with him the whole night when his first girlfriend had dumped him.

Or rather she was kissing him.

Except suddenly she didn't taste like smoke anymore. She tasted like sunshine, strawberries and hot sex. Her hands in his hair, she tugged his lower lip with her teeth. And then swiped over it with an erotic flick of her tongue.

Damn it, where had the girl learned to kiss like that?

Marcus groaned, lust crashing through him. He was kissing Annie and it felt damn good.

Better than good, it felt bloody fantastic.

He pushed her inside and kicked the door closed. No way was he putting on a show for anyone in the town. His hands on her waist, he pushed her towards the right wall.

Her hands twined around his neck, she whimpered as he licked the seam of her lower lip. He swallowed the sound and pushed his tongue inside. And his blood flew south.

He caressed the inside of her mouth and sucked on her tongue. She moved her hands underneath his sweater. A roar thundered in his ears, his muscles tightening from her feathery touch.

Digging his hands into her hair, he trailed a line of hot, open-mouthed kisses down her jaw.

Her hands moved lower and traced his erection.

With a groan, he grabbed her wrists, and pulled them up, his breathing harsh and fast.

He looked into her brown gaze. Arousal and something else he couldn't define, danced in her gaze. It should have felt awkward. It didn't.

The strength of how much he wanted to be here with her, how much he wanted to continue, didn't bother him at all.

"If you touch me, I can't stop, Annie. It's been six months and you taste like heaven and if you touch me…I swear Annie, I won't be able to stop until I'm inside you."

He pressed a fierce kiss again before she could even reply. Just in case she said no, in case this never happened again, and he needed to remember how erotic she tasted.

A smile curved her mouth, the cute little dimple in her right cheek the sexiest he had ever seen. She tugged the zipper on her coat, and threw the bulky thing away.

The long sleeved pink tee was wet and clung to her breasts, the sight of the hard nipples sending another wave of desire roaring through him. His jeans were uncomfortably tight.

She clutched the hem of her tee and plucked it off in one smooth movement. Pink lace fondled small, high breasts. "I don't want you to stop, Marcus," she said, a shy smile curving her lips. Her hands lingered on the waistband of her jeans. "But this is as far as my courage will go."

Something other than lust zigzagged through him but Marcus was too far gone to pay attention to it. With a smile, he made short work of their clothes. Unhooking her bra, he fondled her breasts, unable to wait. Arching her back, she pushed herself into his touch.

It was all the approval Marcus needed. He took her nipple into his mouth and suckled it. Her throaty scream was just enough to push him to the edge. He grabbed a condom from his wallet, pushed his jeans down and pulled it on.

His hands on her waist, he lifted her against the wall, and she wrapped her legs around him.

He pushed her thong out of the way, and pushed into her in one deep thrust.

Their mingled groans rent the room, filling the very air they breathed. Every sinew and muscle in him was taut with the need to move, to thrust into her like a...

"God, Marcus. Please...move... or something," she said, her words slurring on top of each other.

He began a slow rhythm but only by the skin of his teeth. She dug her teeth into his shoulder and bit him, hard. Marcus lost the last ounce of control. A groan fell from his mouth. He increased his pace and thrust deeper and longer into her.

He pressed his mouth to her breast and tugged the nipple softly with his teeth.

She fell apart, the most sensuous sounds falling from her mouth and Marcus thrust one last time.

He looked into her beautiful brown eyes just as pleasure splintered into a million waves in and around him. He saw something in that gaze that tugged at him.

And even the heaven of her tight body wasn't enough to blind him to the shadow of the pain she didn't hide fast enough.

Chapter Three

Marcus was seriously beginning to get pissed off. The day had been one hectic thing after the other. And any free minutes he'd had between that, he had spent trying to locate Annie. Whom he hadn't seen since New Year's Eve two days ago.

By the time, he had woken up the next morning, she had, of course, disappeared. Deciding to give her the space she needed, he had held off. And *waited*.

And he was still waiting.

First, he'd had the sinking thought that she had fled again.

Except wherever he turned, the whole damn village was talking about her. Because everybody in Coombethwaite loved Annie, had missed Annie. More than one guy was excited over her return. The very thought nauseated him now.

So she was avoiding him. And a damn good fireman he was that he couldn't locate a twenty-five-year-old woman in the tiny village.

He made quick work of his sandwich at the village pub. He was just about to step out when he ran into old Mr. Marshall, one of the partners from the local law firm, Morris and Marshall.

"Hey, Marcus. Annie Bennett came to see me this morning. Wanted to lease the bakery to open it again."

So, she *was* back for good. The thought cheered him up no end.

He nodded. "Did you tell her I own the property?"

"No. I said I would let her know in the evening. She's down

there right now, checking out everything. I didn't see any problem in letting her walk around."

"Already? Won't she need an influx of cash to get it going first?"

"Oh, she has everything ready, Marcus. She's putting up a little of her own money and a loan has been approved by the bank for the rest of it. I mean, she practically ran that bakery even before Henry died and it's not like Max of all people was going to refuse her a loan, right?" he said, wiggling his eyebrows, as though it was all very funny.

Marcus didn't think it funny at all. Their slick little banker had had a thing for Annie since they had both been in diapers.

Marcus took off towards the Bennett Bakery. Even though Annie had closed it down when her father died four years ago, and then moved to London, everyone still thought of it as Bennett Bakery.

Apparently, the little minx had everything planned perfectly.

Except he wasn't sure he liked just being an item on her list of risks that was done and crossed off. This time, he wasn't going to stand by and be ignored. Not after what they had shared.

A fresh dose of anger diluted the excitement thrumming through his veins.

But even the anger was a thousand times better than the numbing loneliness of the past three years.

#

Annie made another quick note in her notepad, old memories and new excitement building inside her chest again. The moment she had stepped into her dad's old bakery, she knew she had made the right decision.

This was where she belonged.

Of course, she still had to face Marcus, still had to deal with the consequences of their…

Just thinking about it sent heat cruising to all kinds of places she didn't want to think of in the middle of the day. She still couldn't believe how bold she had been. And how *incredibly good* it had felt. She had done far more than she had dared think even in her wildest dreams.

She couldn't regret it but she was already wondering what the fall-out would be.

Would she lose Marcus's friendship now? How long could she avoid him? Would every conversation between them turn awkward now? Wasn't that why she had held back all these years?

She blew her breath out hard and leant against the wall. Then slithered to the floor like a deflated balloon.

If only she didn't miss him so much.

The niggling fear only solidified in her mind now.

She would always be in love with him.

All she could do now was to accept it and live her life as best as she could.

The view from the floor cheered her up a little.

Whoever had bought the property had taken very good care of it. All she needed was to hire a couple of part-time helpers for the morning baking, install the new billing machine she had bought in London, start ordering supplies again and she would be good to open in a fortnight at the worst.

She started making a list of all the things she needed to do when the front door opened. And there stood Marcus.

He was dressed in blue jeans with a flannel shirt open over a white tee. And he was smiling. The warmth in his gaze was enough to set tingles rollicking all over her skin.

She swallowed and glanced up at him. "Hi."

He joined her on the floor and handed her a brown bag and a bottle of water. "You must be hungry. It's way past lunch time."

Her heart kicked against her ribs.

She mumbled thanks and took the bag with trembling fingers, tears burning at the back of her eyes. Thank God some things didn't change in life.

He sat in silence next to her as she finished her sandwich,

drank half the bottle of water. But nothing could dampen the effect of his nearness on her. The lemon scent of his shampoo, the heat from his body-warmth flooded through her. She tried to keep her gaze on her own hands but they kept drifting to his large, rough ones. And that instantly reminded her of how they had felt on her breasts.

Coils of remembered pleasure heated between her thighs.

"You've been avoiding me."

She straightened, heat singeing her cheeks.

She shook her head. "I've been..." The words stopped as he turned towards her, his gaze eating her up hungrily. She licked her lips, and tried to gather her thoughts. "Marcus, I think it was a bad-"

"It wasn't, Annie. I'll flatten you against the floor right now and show you why it isn't in full view of the village." He stared at her, desire blazing in his gaze. God, she had dreamed so many times of him looking at her like that. "What I can't figure out is why the hell we haven't done it before."

Her mouth dried at the heat in his words.

Because he had always been in love with someone else and she had been too scared of losing him if she let on how she felt.

She stiffened as he clasped her hand in his and kissed the back of it.

She twined her fingers through his, breathed through the pleasure the simple touch incited and looked into his eyes. "I... it was...*it was fantastic*."

A teasing glint appeared in his eyes, his smile playing havoc with her control. His fingers traced lazy circles on the inside of her wrist.

She jerked her hand back. "However, it doesn't mean that we should..." she swallowed as a frown replaced his smile, "we should continue in that vein."

"Why the hell not? Are you seeing someone else?"

She glared right back at him. "Of course not."

"If you're not, then give me one good reason. I like you, you like me and we light up a storm when we touch each other."

She pushed herself onto her knees and hugged him on an impulse. His arms tightened around her, the deafening roar of her heartbeat drowning out everything else. She squeezed her eyes shut, locking back the tears.

His embrace was everything that was perfect and good in her life. Shouldn't she be happy with what she had then?

She leaned back. "I can't afford to lose you, Marcus. You're the only one left in this whole wide world for me. If…*When* things go wrong, as they usually do in these cases, I will lose you and I can't even bear that thought."

"I can never cut you out like you did these four years. Whatever happens between us—"

"I'm not willing to take that risk."

"Ahhh…I see." Hardness entered his usually carefree gaze. "So you're back to being boring, dependable, un-risking Annie again then?"

She fell back onto her haunches with a soft thud, waves of hurt barrelling through her. It was exactly what she had always thought of herself. And yet hearing it from his mouth was a thousand times worse.

"Or that wasn't even an actual risk, was it?" he continued, anger pouring out of his stiff body. "How stupid was I to think it was something special?"

He'd thought it special. Then why was he ruining it?

She glared at him, letting the anger that followed wash through her. She shoved him back with both hands. Not that, God of Well-Defined Muscles that he was, he budged even an inch. "You've turned into a jerk, Crowley," she said, using his last name as she had done so many times whenever they had a fight.

She had a sinking sensation that this was one fight they couldn't just get over.

"You think I came onto you because it was New Year's Eve

or because I was on the rebound from my ex? I've wanted to kiss you for so long, Marcus. Except I always had maybe a few seconds between your breakups and the time you found a new girlfriend again, to make my move."

He stepped back from her, his face tilted to the side, his gaze studying her curiously. "What the hell, Annie? You never said a thing."

"Well, it's a good thing, seeing that I've acted on it and we're fighting now, isn't it?"

Without a word, he rose to his feet and gave her a hand up. His mouth was narrowed tight, his anger vibrated from him. "See, you might not have used me as rebound— which frankly, I'm beginning to like a lot better than this." He waved his hands between them, "but you had time to think through all this. You decided what it was going to be, how long it would last. You made up all the rules, without taking my feelings into consideration.

You just played it out like one of those imaginary games you used to love playing. And at the end of the game, you always ended up alone, didn't you? Hope you enjoy it this time too."

He pulled a sheaf of papers from his pocket and threw them at the glass display case. "Here's the lease agreement for the bakery. Put whatever the hell you want on it and deal with Mr. Marshall."

"You? You bought the bakery? Why?"

"Because I always hoped you would come back one day." His mouth narrowed tight, he ran a hand through his hair. "Welcome home, Annie."

Chapter Four

The following week, Annie worked from dawn to dusk, leaving herself no time to even think about Marcus. She hired a part-time helper for the mornings when the bakery opened, ordered a boatload of inventory, and started experimenting with some new recipes she had designed for the menu.

But apparently, her mind could function completely apart from what her body was doing and quite well at that. Even through the exhausting, thorough cleaning she had decided to give the place without help.

Because all she could think of was the resentment in Marcus's gaze, the cutting disappointment in his words as though she had cheated him, shattered his trust. And by now, she was convinced he had been right.

The rag with which she had been polishing the glass front of the bakery slipped from her fingers. She leaned her forehead against it as the realization set in.

Marcus had been right.

She hadn't really taken a risk that night, had she? More like, she had stuck her nose out into the cold, enjoyed the cold and then went screaming back inside.

She had only wanted to protect herself from hurt. It was all she had ever done since her mother died. Made sure she never risked anything that might end up hurting her.

And instead she had hurt Marcus through her own selfishness.

Exhaling a shaky breath, she picked up the rag, threw it onto the pile and headed for the toilet in the back.

Within minutes, she bundled herself up in her coat, pulled on her mittens and cap and set off towards the pub. It was almost time for dinner, and she would definitely find Marcus over there. If not, she would just continue on to his cottage.

The chilly air nipped at her nose but she kept walking. And she closed her to mind to any speculation it wanted to indulge in as to what she would say once she found him.

Her gut still felt bottomless though.

#

Marcus picked up the drink from the dark wood bar at the King's Head and walked back to the booth, preferring to drink alone rather than with his fellow firemen downing pints on the other side. The pub was full tonight, laughter and shouts filling the air around them. It was the last place he wanted to be, but for once, he didn't want to be alone at home either.

He took a sip of his drink when Molly, the new elementary school teacher, smiled at him a foot away. He nodded back.

Molly had a sweet smile and she obviously liked him. The way she was always finding excuses to touch him or talk to him left him in no doubt. She was available and she didn't have any hang ups about it. Just the kind of fun-loving, uncomplicated woman he liked. Because that's the kind of man he was.

If he wanted something, he went after it, he didn't analyze it to death, he didn't put everyone else's wishes before his own... In short, he had always been a selfish bastard.

Oblivious to everything else around him too, apparently. How else could he have missed the fact that Annie had been attracted to him? How could he have missed it?

He was so lost in thought it took him a minute to respond when Molly neared and asked if she could join him. He nodded without thinking.

Suddenly, she was squeezing next to him on his side of the

booth, much too close for comfort.

It took Marcus exactly ten seconds to realize he had zero interest in her. She had the wrong color eyes, she hung onto every word he said with a smile, her smile was too sweet…

In short, she wasn't Annie.

Whether having a silent meal, or looking at the stars, or kissing until his blood thrummed with desire, he wanted to do it only with Annie. And he didn't even fight the realization. Hell, what was there to fight about?

What he and Annie shared, *whatever it was*, was worth a fighting chance, was something that didn't come by too often. If they didn't, he would never know what might have been. He would always wonder.

And nothing that happened between them would make him love her any less than he already did. Nothing could change that.

He felt excitement rush through his blood again. All he needed was to convince Annie that he was worth the risk.

He was just about to spin some story about having to leave early when Molly bent towards him and pressed her mouth to his.

Shock spiraled through him. Tightening his fists by his sides so that he didn't push her away, as every nerve in him wanted to, he waited for Molly to be done kissing him.

It was pleasant, she smelled nice and tasted good. But nothing like the blaze of fireworks that had erupted in his mouth when Annie had kissed him, nothing that would make him weak in the knees and craving more.

Nothing that would make his gut ache when he woke up tomorrow.

Her blue gaze flying open, Molly pulled back. "Nope, huh?"

He smiled ruefully. "Sorry, Molly."

She smiled, stretched up on her toes and leaned in close. "Would it have anything to do with the woman standing at the entrance glaring at you with barely concealed disgust?"

A shiver ran down Marcus's spine even before he turned. Annie stood at the entrance, her hands stuck in her coat pockets, her gorgeous hair pushed back under her silly cap.

Across the pub, amidst the voices and laughter around them, he could see the tight set of her mouth, her eyes glimmering with unshed tears. Tension poured out from her.

Every inch of him wanted to rush across the room and grab hold of her before she did a one-eighty again. Instead, he forced himself to turn his gaze away from Annie, and bent towards Molly, who watched them with interest.

"Please play along, Molly," he whispered, and the blonde nodded, her gaze twinkling merrily.

By the time he turned his gaze towards the entrance again, Annie had taken several steps in.

The tension between them must have been more obvious than he had thought because suddenly, a hush fell over the crowd around them. Damn it, the last thing he wanted was the whole town's attention on him and Annie.

Annie reached them in quick steps, a lone tear sliding down one cheek.

The breath knocked out of him, Marcus moved towards her. He never, ever wanted to hurt her.

"Annie, before—"

Curiously, she slid her upper body sideways. To get a look at Molly, he slowly realized.

"Please don't take this wrongly, Molly," Annie said in a crystal clear voice that reverberated around the hushed room. "I've only heard the nicest things about you and I'm sure we'll be great friends soon."

Apparently satisfied with her statement, because, of course, Annie would die rather than hurt anyone, she turned towards him.

Fire sparkled in her brown eyes. Her delicate jaw wobbled as she took a deep breath. "You could only wait one week?" Her words hitched on a sob, and every muscle in Marcus's body tightened with tension. "You slept with me, told me what we had was worth taking a chance on, and then just when I convinced myself you were right, here you are, kissing another woman?"

He clamped his hand over her arm, determined to explain, but not with an audience.

She jerked back from him, her tears running freely now.

And Marcus never, not in a million years, saw the punch that clocked his jaw, coming.

She was gone, disappeared from the bar in the two seconds he took to recover from her neatly delivered blow.

Damn if the woman couldn't land a fine one.

He grabbed his jacket and turned towards the entrance. Most of his own crew, joined by every well-meaning biddy from the town, blocked his way, their collective wrath a palpable thing.

Ignoring the rest, he focused on his friend, Nick, the one he was closest to. Meaning he hung out with him more than anyone else. Because, truly, Annie was the only one he had ever been really close with. And damn if he ever let go of that.

Even if he had to spend the rest of his life convincing her of it.

He felt the hard knot in his chest melt away at the simple realization. That's what he wanted. He wanted to spend the rest of his life with her. He couldn't let her slip away again.

Except, she probably hated him now. A second knot took the place of the first one.

"Leave her alone, Marcus," came the first warning.

He gritted his teeth, ready to take on the whole lot of them the way he was feeling. "Look, guys, this is really none of your business."

Nick cleared his throat. "It is, Marcus. It's high time you knew this. If you had stayed away from her—"

Marcus frowned. "Jesus, Nick. I would never do anything

to—"

"God, Marcus, you still don't see it, don't you? Annie's been in love with you for God knows how long."

Marcus staggered back as Nick paused. Shock drifted through him slowly, and he cursed.

"Maybe forever. She knows it, the whole damn town knows it, even Grace knew it. Only you didn't. So, even if you didn't mean to hurt her, I think you already have."

He felt as if a fog was slowly lifting away from his eyes.

And Marcus was just as terrified at the prospect of losing it as he was excited at his discovery.

Chapter Five

She was not going to run away again.

Shaking her right fist to ease its throbbing, Annie pulled the covers back and slid into her bed. So what if the whole town had been witness to her breakdown? This was her home now. She refused to leave. Maybe, Marcus would do the gentlemanly thing for once and leave instead.

That thought didn't bring the cheer she thought it would.

She plumped her pillow and stared up at the ceiling, tears not far away again.

The door to the bedroom opened with a creak. She jerked upright in the bed as a long shadow slipped into the room. She was just about to scream to high-heaven when the room flooded with light.

She blinked, her jaw hanging open.

Marcus leaned against the closed door. And he didn't seem in a pleasant mood. In fact, he looked downright furious.

She fell back to the bed, intent on ignoring both the thump-thump of her heart *and* him.

"Go away, Marcus. I have nothing to say to you."

She had no idea that such a big man could move so stealthily. She smelled the tangy scent of him, and stiffened. The old bed squeaked and grumbled as he lowered his huge frame onto the bed.

She jerked her sheet upwards. With the brute lying on top of it, it didn't move.

With a grunt, she pushed up on her elbows and dared a glance his way.

Wrong move.

His blue gaze devoured her, the intensity in it sending tingles all the way to her toes.

He moved to his side. "I wasn't out on a date with Molly. You owe me an apology."

The ground slipped from under Annie. Her heart began racing again. This way, she was going to end up with a heart problem. "She kissed you," she managed to say.

Heat radiated from his huge body and swathed her like a blanket. "*She* was kissing *me*, Annie. I wasn't." He threw an arm over her casually. Her body instantly went into melt-down mode. "I only want to kiss you."

Her stomach fluttered at the raspy need in his tone. "I…I'm sorry, Marcus." She licked her lips and turned towards him. "I'll apologize in front of the whole town if you want."

His brow tied into a fierce frown, his gaze didn't budge from her. "Apparently, the town's cleverer than I give it credit for."

A slow churn began in the pit of her stomach. God, she knew where this was going. "What do you mean?" She pushed the question past her throat with the utmost effort.

His hand moved up over her torso, toward her face. Somehow, some time in the last few minutes, he had wedged in closer to her. His rock-solid muscles rubbed just the tiniest bit against her side. His long fingers cupped her jaw, his arm a heavy weight between her breasts.

She had nowhere to look but into the depths of those blue eyes that she had loved for so long.

"Is it true?"

She felt like she was standing on the edge of an abyss. This was it. Either she could lay her heart on the line, risk it all, or live with constant regret that she hadn't even tried. That she didn't consider her own happiness worth the risk.

She bobbed her head up and down. She just couldn't form a simple 'yes'.

Warmth exploded in his eyes. He tugged her hard against him and buried his face in the curve of her neck. His body was a taut mass of hard muscles against hers. It was heaven, it was hell and it was exactly where she wanted to be. "God, Annie, I don't deserve it."

She had a suspicion he was trying to recover his composure.

She ran her hands over his back, finding a strange exhilaration in the truth. How could she have held back from this for so long?

Just this moment with Marcus, his breath mingling with hers, the tenderness in his gaze was worth so much.

She pressed her lips to his strong jaw and kissed him. "It's always been you, Marcus. And how could I not love you? Any moment of joy in my life, any moment worth remembering, you brought it into my life. How could I not fall in love with you?"

His blue gaze was filled with such tenderness that her heart overflowed with love.

"Will you forgive me for being a thickheaded idiot?"

He didn't wait for an answer.

He dipped his head and kissed her. A whimper tearing out of her throat, Annie felt the heat of his kiss flare out all over her skin in tiny, infinite tingles. His mouth nipped at her lips, his tongue swiping over her with an erotic mastery that had her craving for more.

It was a long, drugging kiss that had her pulling the hem of his shirt over his head. She whistled in appreciation, her gaze devouring the hard muscles. She wanted to touch him everywhere, she wanted to lick him...

He laughed loudly and she realized she had spoken her thoughts aloud. He locked her hands with his. "You are cutting off the speech I prepared," he teased her.

"So the choice is your words or your body?"

She eyed the man's rippling torso. A smile splitting her mouth, she scrunched her nose. "God, Marcus. I've had erotic dreams about what I would do with your body just as much as I've dreamed of hearing you say those words. Not a fair choice then, is it?"

In answer, he pulled the covers back from her in a swift move. And tugged the hem of her spaghetti-strapped top down. "Then how about I alternate kissing and talking?"

He pressed an open mouthed kiss to her shoulder. "I love you, Annie."

She laughed and cried.

He pulled the top down a little more, baring her breast. Color bled into his cheeks, hunger stamped onto his features. "I want to spend the rest of my life with you."

He dragged his face down the side of her breast.

Annie shuddered as pleasure zoomed across her skin.

"I want you to marry me so that I can kiss you and tell you how much I love you every single day."

His gaze still on her, he opened his mouth and closed it over a nipple.

She screamed and bucked off the bed.

"Is that a yes?" he asked and she nodded, giving herself over to a lifetime of pleasure and love.

About the author:

Tara Pammi had her nose stuck in a romance novel for as long as she could remember. Until one day, she decided to write one herself and hasn't looked back. Tara lives in Colorado, USA with her very own hero, two daughters and dreams of kicking the dayjob to the curb one of these days. You can connect with her on twitter @Sri_Tara.

Books by Tara
A Hint of Scandal (The Sensational Stanton Sisters – Book 1)
A Touch of Temptation (The Sensational Stanton Sisters)

A Kindling Romance

Lorraine Wilson

Chapter One

This. Was. Not. Happening.

"Oh dear, what can the matter be? Polly and puss are stuck up the chimney."

Polly Minton couldn't get the rhyme out of her head. It was official. She was going loopy.

She braced her back against the cold Lakeland stone and stroked the tiny tabby kitten curled up in a ball against her chest, in an attempt to ward off the rising hysteria.

The kitten's tiny razor claws hooked into her very sooty towelling dressing gown. With luck, the stroking would calm herself as well as the cat. She desperately needed distraction from the claustrophobia lurking at the corners of her mind, just waiting to strike.

So this was where being neighbourly got you.

She took a deep breath, attempting to relax the muscles in her rigid chest. This couldn't be happening. She should be next door slipping into her silky Ghost dress and making her way to the New Year's dinner at Coombethwaite Hotel, not stuck up Mrs Cromaty's chimney.

The partners at Morris and Marshall would not be impressed if she turned up late. Tonight was about schmoozing potential clients for the firm, earning her stripes. Proving that hiring a city girl had been a good idea.

"I've called the fire brigade, dear." Mrs Cromaty's voice sounded oddly distorted through the chimney shaft. The

Lakeland stone was thick, muffling chunks of solid rock—No, she couldn't let herself think about that…

"Okay, thanks," Polly tried to sound if not cheerful then at least brave, as though she didn't mind a bit being covered with soot and scraped by the rough stone.

Not to mention being well and truly stuck.

How would they get her out? Panic rose in her chest and she gulped it down, practicing her yoga breathing.

Breathe in. One, two, three, four. Hold. One, two, three, four…

If she'd come up she should, in theory, be able to get back down again.

Breathe out. One, two, three, four.

Her head swam and she struggled to keep her balance on the ledge. Perhaps she'd overdone the deep breathing.

"Is Tabitha okay?" Mrs Cromaty asked.

"Yes, I think I've calmed her down a bit. How long has she been up here? She feels a bit thin."

"Three days. She went up the chimney when I bought her home from the rescue centre, so I've had no chance to feed her up. The RSPCA man said to put food down at the grate and she'd come down when she was good and ready." Her voice took on an indignant tone. "It's alright for them with their central heating. Don't they realise I've only the open fire to keep me warm?"

"It's okay, Mrs Cromaty, I'm sure I'll be out of your chimney soon and we can light your fire," Polly shouted back. Then she bit her lip, she wasn't sure at all. Why oh why had she answered the knock at the door instead of staying in her nice warm bath?

She felt the fragility of the little warm bundle cuddled into her chest and sighed; she couldn't have left the kitten up here. The little tabby must have been Mrs C's fifth or was it sixth rescue cat? Very commendable, but it would be tonight of all nights that her neighbour needed help.

Polly should have considered all the extra mince pies she'd

eaten over Christmas before trying to squeeze up the crooked, ancient chimney.

How would they get her out? When her sister was eight years old she'd trapped her finger in a wrought iron bench and the fire brigade had greased her finger with butter... They didn't still do that, did they? Oh the indignity.

Shifting her position on the rocky ledge, Polly tried to get more comfortable. Grade II listed chimneys were all very well but whoever built this one must have been drunk on medieval ale. How would she ever live this down? She might be a Londoner but she knew how small communities worked—her adventure would be all over the village before the week was out, spread from the post office by the very talkative postman.

Some fresh start this was turning out to be!

Groaning, she squeezed her eyes tight shut. Maybe I can just play dead, open my eyes when it's all over and have a convenient memory blank...

Perhaps she should go back to London, join the trail of dissatisfied 'Escape to the Country' refugees now returning to their natural habitat of concrete and traffic jams.

No, not that!

She was surprised by the strength of her instant reaction, but knew the instinct was right. She was done with London and the pressurised city lawyer jobs that squeezed out every drop of life from her. She liked being able to see the skyline and loved inhaling fresh air in the mornings as she gazed across the estuary to Coombe Mountain. She was still getting over the shock of complete strangers stopping her in the street just to say hello...

Polly lowered her head to the tabby, nuzzling her nose against the soft fur. The cat clearly needed a bath, well didn't they both! But the contact was comforting, a link to a living being, something that needed her. Maybe she should get a cat? Perhaps Mrs C might let her take Tabitha home. Despite struggling when Polly had first grabbed her, the kitten barely stirred now as they waited.

"Are you playing dead too, little tabby Tabitha?" she whispered. The walls of the chimneybreast seemed to be closing in, squeezing out her breath. Tears pricked at the back of her eyes and she blinked them away.

Get a grip Polly, brave face and all that.

"The fire brigade are here now, dear," Mrs Cromaty called up the chimney.

Hope and dread simultaneously flooded Polly. She fought the urge to bang her head against the cold Lakeland stone. There was the sound of heavy footsteps below.

"Hi there," Polly called out, forcing a smile into her voice.

Chapter Two

Drew Reynolds frowned and stopped in his tracks, scratching at his stubble. Was that a voice coming from the chimney? He'd definitely only had the one drink at the pub. Even though it was New Year, he was on call and was always very careful to stay below the limit.

"Er, Enid." He turned to see the old lady stroking a black and white cat. "You did say you had a cat up the chimney, didn't you?"

"Of course." She stared as though he were a bit simple.

"Only I could have sworn I just heard a voice up there."

"Oh, that'll be the girl who's moved in next door. She tried to help but," she lowered her tone to a whisper, "the daft lass has gone and got herself stuck."

Drew's heart plummeted to the bottom of his boots. "It's just if you'd told me it wasn't only a cat that was stuck I would have brought the crew—made the call official."

"They'll all be in the King's Head, no doubt." Enid pursed her lips.

Drew ignored the jibe. The crew needed to relax tonight but he wasn't about to start justifying anything to Enid. He knew they would all stay under the limit until midnight when they were technically no longer on call. "All I've got is this." He pulled the packet of smoked salmon out of his deep coat pocket and rolled his eyes.

The scorn in Enid's eyes made him feel like the small boy he'd been when he first met her at the village show.

The Cromaty Cat Callouts had become so frequent in recent years it hardly seemed fair to ruin the crew's New Year's Eve. There'd been a particularly gruesome call out last week and they'd had to cut someone they knew out of the wreckage caused by a drunk driver. They needed to unwind tonight. Personally, Drew hated New Year's Eve. He preferred to keep busy and he'd always had the knack when it came to extracting cats from odd hiding places. He'd even earned the jokey nickname of The Cat Whisperer. As for women, they were a different breed and he was out of practice.

Enid wrinkled her nose at the smoked salmon. "I don't think that will get the lass down, do you?"

Drew bit back a retort and took a deep breath. It was time to take charge of the situation. He moved over to the wide chimneybreast and crouched, sticking his head up into the darkness. "Hi there, what's your name?"

"Polly," she called down, a catch in her voice betraying her anxiety.

"Okay Polly, my name's Drew. Are you stuck?"

"Of course I'm bloody stuck." Indignation overcame fear. "Do you think I do this for a hobby?"

Drew knew how to deal with panic. She needed distracting. On reflection, it had been a daft question to ask, but experience on the job had taught him never to make assumptions. Sometimes human beings did very odd things when they were ill or under pressure.

He crouched, feeling the wall for any loose stones, analysing the width of the shaft. "You know, if you're delivering presents you're about a week late."

He peered up and could just about make out a dim figure, feet wedged on either side above the hole, cradling something to her chest.

"Ha, ha. Look, are you sure you're a real fireman? I don't mean to be picky but how are you going to get me out?" A slight quaver at the end of the question gave her away.

She was terrified.

"Don't worry Polly, I'll get you out, I promise. And yes, I am a real fireman, a retained firefighter from Coombethwaite station."

Drew rubbed the back of his neck. Mrs Cromaty's house was a grade II listed property and there would be hell to pay if he tried anything structural. But if Polly had gone up she could come down, he would just have to coax her. Perhaps it wasn't that different from a cat rescue after all.

Polly's quiet voice came from the chimney. "What's your plan?"

"Pass the cat down."

Drew reached up through the hole and a soft, wriggly bundle was placed into his hands. It was light, little more than a kitten. Sharp claws punctured his hands but he didn't flinch, just gently carried the cat to Enid whose sharp composure softened at the sight of the cat.

"Take the cat into the kitchen so it can't dart back up the chimney." He crouched down in the hearth.

"So Polly, if you managed to squeeze up there in the first place then you know logically you can come back down, right?"

"I s'pose," she sniffed.

"Lower your legs first," he spoke more gently, "but stop before your hips reach the narrowest part of the shaft."

A slim pair of bare, shapely ankles slid out of the hole.

Oh boy, it was going to take every ounce of self-control to stay professional on this job.

"I'm going to take your weight for a moment, okay?"

Her reply was inaudible but he firmly grabbed her calves anyway. She stopped dead.

"Keep coming and when we get to your hips I'll tell you how to control your breath. You're going to need to take a deep breath in and then expel all the air from your body."

She didn't respond and didn't move.

"What's wrong?"

"My dressing gown will get stuck."

She was wearing a dressing gown?

"I was getting ready to go out when Mrs Cromaty knocked on my door," a small voice said, as though Polly had heard his thoughts.

"Well, you'll have to leave it up there and we can bring it down afterwards. It will give you a bit more room," he responded, remarkably patiently considering his thighs were beginning to strain in their unnatural position in the hearth.

"Couldn't you just make the hole wider?" she pleaded. "Haven't you brought cutting equipment?"

"Destroy a grade II listed, five-hundred-year-old chimney just to spare your modesty? No, I'm afraid not. So unless you plan on seeing in the New Year up Enid's chimney, you're going to have to do what's necessary."

He added more kindly, "Don't worry, it's just me and Enid down here."

Polly sighed and wriggled above him, as if releasing herself from the dressing gown. She lowered her weight down into his arms. As predicted, he struggled to keep his thoughts professional as her thighs appeared through the hole. Then suddenly she stopped, resisting his gentle but persuasive tug, jerking swiftly back upwards.

"I can't, I just don't fit. I've already tried." Her words were a panicked staccato. "I'm terrified of getting stuck in the hole."

"Like Winnie the Pooh?" He remembered the story he read to his nephews.

A snort of jerky laughter told him he was succeeding in pulling her back from the edge of fear. Phobias were funny things to anyone not actually experiencing them. Odd, but horribly powerful and they took careful handling.

"Enid could always use your legs as a clothes horse," he joked.

"I think she'd rather have her fire back."

"Listen, Polly. Trust me. Ease yourself down gently. There's no rush, I'm here for as long as it takes."

"I'm claustrophobic."

"I guessed," he replied gently. "I will get you out, I promise."

Chapter Three

Polly swallowed down the hysteria and tried to control her breathing again. Drew's voice was having an oddly calming effect. He sounded so sure of himself, assuredly in control, his voice so incredibly deep and...sexy.

Where did that come from? It must just be the surge in adrenalin. Still, the knowledge she was about to slide into his arms wearing nothing but her underwear made her feel rather odd.

Best undies and a whole pile of soot, really attractive, Polly!

"I'm sorry, have I ruined your night out?" She tried to buy herself some more time.

"Not at all. I'm not a great fan of New Year's Eve to be honest."

Was he just being polite? He certainly sounded sincere, a down-to-earth guy. When had she last met one of those?

"Me neither." Her fears escaped in quickly blurted words. "Promise me something, Drew."

"What?"

"Promise you're not filming me on your mobile and this isn't going to be all over YouTube in the morning?" Polly was dimly aware her question was insulting. This guy was a professional and rules were rules, even out here in the sticks.

"Trust me," the calm, deep voice replied.

Something in the warm tone and the firm grip on her legs made her want to do exactly that. She felt she might do anything he asked.

Anything at all.

"You won't have to cover me in butter?" she gabbled, and then added, in case he thought she was a weirdo, "My sister got her hand stuck once and the fire-brigade put butter on her."

"Not unless you want me to." There was a hint of amusement in his reply, a very brief flicker of a flirt. Or had she imagined it?

Sexual desire shivered through her body. It had been a long time since anyone had made her feel like this and she didn't even know what Drew looked like. It was that deep, sexy voice...

He must have really powerful pheromones if they were working on her through the thick Lakeland stone.

"So, do you still use butter?" Polly said, desperate to put off the moment she gave squeezing down the shaft another go.

"We've progressed to olive oil now. Fewer calories."

Funny as well as sexy, hmmm.

"Very funny." Despite herself, Polly smiled in the darkness. Although she felt her cheeks burn at the thought of him slathering her with oil, running those firm fingers over her body until she was slick and slippery in his arms.

Come on Polly, get on with it.

"I'll try again." She lowered herself down, trying not to flinch as he grasped her thighs, taking her weight.

"Okay, now take a deep breath in, all the way down to your diaphragm."

She obeyed.

"Hold it, then slowly expel all the air from your lungs and pull your tummy in. Imagine George Clooney has just walked into the room. Now push down, I've got you."

Never mind George Clooney—Polly was pretty interested to see what Drew was like. Anyway, she couldn't imagine George getting himself sooty for her.

She squeezed down, trusting him, but then her hips wedged against the stone and she panicked, tensing up. On scrambling up to rescue Tabitha, she hadn't given the narrowness of the chimney a moment's thought, had just responded to the thought of a poor rescue cat, frightened and starving up there.

"Hey, relax." Drew's voice sounded muffled.

Polly forced herself to think about him, trying to trust him.

But another insistent voice pressed in—I'm stuck, I'm stuck, I'm stuck...

"It's okay, I've got you." The light squeeze he gave her legs was doubtless meant as a gesture of reassurance, but instead increased her agitation, setting her heart pounding.

"Oh, right. Thanks, Enid, we'll give it a try." Drew's voice was different now, more matter of fact and clipped.

His breath was warm against her cold skin when he spoke again. "She's... um, brought some butter. You know, it would be a better idea than a chainsaw and might be less stressful if it helps you out faster..."

"Just get me out of here and then lose whatever report you're supposed to file at the bottom of Coombethwaite Lake."

He laughed. "I'll see what I can do. Try to push back up a bit."

Polly squeezed back up through the hole an inch, and then felt a warm liquid feeling squirming in the pit of her stomach. It matched the soft butter Drew was sliding over her lower back. His hand slid over her thighs. At first in a methodical manner and then, gradually his strokes became rhythmic as he circled up into the shaft, studiously ignoring the elastic edge of her fancy knickers. He covered her lower hips and tried to coat the base of her spine without actually touching her bottom.

The situation drove her mad. The more appropriate he tried to be, the more she wanted his fingers everywhere. Despite her panic and the ludicrous situation, she was growing wet between her legs and very, very turned on.

"Okay?"

She swallowed. "Yes."

"I'm just going to have to..."

His fingers were on the elastic of her knickers and for one moment she wondered if he were going to insist she take those off too.

In one expert movement he smeared butter over the fabric, so quickly she barely registered his touch.

The unreality of the situation detached her from her normal inhibitions. With insides that had turned to jelly and cheeks burning fiercely, she fought to control the passion rippling through her body. At least he couldn't see the blush or imagine what was going through her mind right now. She would just have to emigrate once this was over. There was no other choice.

"Okay," Drew's tone was brisk. "Let's try again."

With no further warning he grasped her thighs and tugged smartly down, taking her breath away and giving her no time to panic.

She collapsed in a messy, sooty heap against him and for a brief moment they lay tangled on the floor on Enid Cromaty's hearthrug.

For the first time, she stared into the warm hazel brown eyes of her rescuer. They creased at the edges as he smiled and a vivid sense of connection winded her. She'd read about this kind of instant connection – le coup de foudre, a thunderbolt, but she'd never experienced it before now. He felt...familiar, like she'd known him forever.

He blinked and then shifted away, pulling himself upright.

Dimly Polly became aware of the fact she was sitting on the floor in only her underwear and a grimy covering of soot and butter. She crossed her arms over her chest, pulled her knees up to her body and stared resolutely at the floor. "Well this is awkward."

"Would you like to borrow this?" He took off his jacket and offered it to her. The t-shirt he wore revealed the rock hard muscles that had held her so effectively.

"Thanks." She wrapped it smartly around her, glad it came down to mid-thigh.

This isn't a real intimacy, it's just an...odd situation. We've been thrown together.

So why had it felt more natural to be almost naked with this man that it did now that she was covered up? Had they been thrown together or brought together?

"I know you said you didn't mind but I'm sorry I've ruined your New Year's Eve." Did he have a date waiting for him in some pub? She couldn't stop staring, mesmerised by the amber specks in his eyes, analysing his laughter lines and scars. She wanted to reach out and stroke the strong jaw-line, to be held in those arms...

"I'm really not bothered about New Year's Eve." He shrugged.

"Really? I thought it was a huge deal in the village, a pub crawl of the village's four pubs and then fireworks in the square? I heard some local bigwig puts on a huge display each year." She carried on talking, not wanting the intimacy to end, needing far more.

"That would be me actually." He grimaced. "It's a tradition. My father always used to do it and so I carry it on."

"I think I was supposed to meet you tonight."

Drew's eyes widened.

Polly flushed. "No, not like that. I mean I was getting ready for the ball at the Coombethwaite hotel. I've just started at Morris and Marshall's and the partners said I needed to schmooze the local VIPs."

"Oh, the ball? I always get the invite but never go. Well not since...not for a long time." Drew grimaced again.

Polly wished she'd never mentioned it.

"I prefer the atmosphere at the Rose and Crown or The King's Head," he said. "It's more relaxed, more me."

He held her gaze and all the tense muscles in her body slowly relaxed. There was an unmistakable message in those eyes—he didn't want tonight to end here either. There might be something to salvage from the ashes of the evening. Literally.

"I'll be in trouble for not turning up. Great impression, eh?" To be fair, a part of her was glad she wasn't there. She'd much rather be here, with Drew. Although not looking such a state, obviously.

"Well, you have met and schmoozed with me." He grinned, quirking an eyebrow as her cheeks grew even hotter. "I'll drop in on Monday and tell them what a good impression you made."

"Um…thanks."

She startled at a crash from the kitchen, and stumbled to her feet. "I guess I'd better go next door and clean myself up so you can have your jacket back. I'm not sure there's any point going to the dinner now, they'll be on the coffees and I can't face explaining where I've been."

Chapter Four

"Why not come to the King's Head with me?" The words were out of Drew's mouth before he knew it. "I mean, you're new to the village, so it would be a shame if you missed the fireworks. You can't see New Year in on your own."

And if you go home I can't kiss you.

He didn't want the evening to end here. It was the first New Year's Eve since Rosa died that he actually wanted to share with anyone. He knew what it was like to be suddenly alone, be it by choice or by fate, and he didn't want to leave Polly alone in her cottage.

Something almost magnetic drew him to her. Well, something besides the obviously stunning curves in all the right places.

He swallowed hard, remembering running his fingers over her flesh. With luck, she hadn't guessed at the unprofessional thoughts galloping through his mind this evening. He'd done his best to keep things professional, although he could probably get away with not logging this. After all it had been a cat call-out and Enid, never understanding procedure, had rung Coombethwaite Manor instead of the fire station. She always called Drew, even when he wasn't on duty. He'd been the victim of his own success as a cat-whisperer.

"Are you sure you don't need to file a report at the fire station?" Polly's eyes stared earnestly into his.

"I can always tell them you were detained helping me rescue a cat. It is the truth after all. There's no need to publicise the...the other part."

"But what about Enid?" Polly whispered, hugging her arms around her, hope sparking in her blue eyes. Her sooty auburn hair was wild around her shoulders. She looked incredibly sexy in his jacket. He tried not to think about the fact she only had underwear on beneath it.

Drew glanced towards the kitchen and then moved closer, pressing his mouth against her ear. "She's so batty no one believes what she says and she only really cares about the cats anyway. It can be our secret."

He felt her shudder, saw her pupils dilating into black pools of desire.

Without any conscious thought or decision to cross a line, they were kissing. Who had moved first? He hardly knew. He only knew he wanted this woman, in a way he hadn't since he'd lost Rosa. He'd had sex since, sure, but not a connection, not passion. Not a desire that felt it would rip him apart.

For the first time he kissed without comparing the kiss to those he had shared with his late wife.

This was all about Polly.

His jacket had fallen open and he ran his thumb over her silk covered breasts, feeling the hard buds of her nipples. For that moment he didn't care about the soot, the impropriety or the old bat in the kitchen.

Polly pushed against his hand, her breath coming in hard, sharp bursts as she leaned against him, her lips against his cheek, hand pressed flat against his chest as though she were checking he was real.

With a supreme effort of will, he pulled back before the point of no return. He jerked away and tugged the edges of his jacket back into place, covering her up.

Just in time. Enid walked back into the room carrying a very wet and cross Tabitha.

"I've just bathed her and she could do with a nice fire to

warm herself up."

Just then Tabitha launched herself out of Enid's arms and dashed for the chimney again.

Drew dived towards the hearth, grabbing her just in time.

"I don't know what to do," Enid sighed. "I can't be doing with boarding my chimney up. I can't have central heating put in. I'm not made of money."

"I can take her if you like?" Polly offered.

Quite generous of her, considering Enid hadn't even acknowledged her efforts.

"There's a wood burning stove in my living room and a metal plate preventing any escape up the chimney. The heating is on, so she can warm up next to a radiator."

Enid eyed her quizzically, for longer than felt comfortable, as though assessing her suitability as a cat owner by mystical means. "I daresay Tabitha would be happy with you. She's taken to you right enough. Now, why don't you go home with her and get cleaned up and we'll see if your man here is as good at starting fires as he's supposed to be at putting them out. I'll send him round for his jacket when he's done." There was a triumphant gleam in Enid's eyes, as though she had engineered the whole thing and knew exactly what they'd been up to.

The uncharitable thought that in previous centuries she would have been called a witch crossed Drew's mind.

Polly's gaze flickered briefly to his, a message in their depths that she wanted him as much as he wanted her. He knelt to get the kindling as she scooped up the cat and left the room, her cheeks crimson beneath the patches of soot.

Chapter Four

Polly showered the grime from her skin, revelling in the warmth, soothed by the jets sluicing her skin clean. Tabitha curled up into a tiny ball on the bath mat next to the heated towel rail and slept.

As she sponged shower gel into her body, her skin tingled.

All she could think was Drew, Drew, Drew... How long would he be? Did he want to take things further? Would he think her dreadful if she wanted to take them further tonight?

Long months of celibacy made her want to throw caution to the wind. Her body craved him with an intensity she'd never felt before. She'd been so far gone when he was kissing her she would have let him do anything he wanted, right there on Mrs Cromaty's hearthrug. No one had ever made her forget herself like that before.

It wasn't just the gentle, masterful way he had prised her out of the chimney, although the sensation of his fingers sliding over her flesh was powerfully fresh in her mind. She jolted with a sharp shiver of pleasure and anticipation. There was something in his eyes—a like soul searching for something life affirming, wanting to experience passion, to make a connection.

She ran the sponge between her legs, wishing he were in the shower with her.

The doorbell chimed and she started. Heart pounding, she leapt out of the shower and grabbed a towel, splashing water on an indignant Tabitha.

Mouth dry, she opened the door to Drew, noticing for the

first time the soot smeared on his face and peppering his dark, closely cropped hair.

They stared wordlessly for what felt like an eternity. Then the corner of Drew's mouth quirked into a smile.

Polly smiled back, her mind made up. "Would you like to use my shower? After all, it's my fault you're covered in soot. I just have to shampoo my hair."

Drew stepped inside and shut the door. "Perhaps I could join you?"

He tugged gently at the towel tucked around her and she let it fall, walking away naked towards the stairs. "Come on then."

A strange calm filled her. She should be worrying about him thinking her a harlot, but surprisingly she wasn't. This felt right, and she was going to enjoy it. Moving to the Lake District had been about choosing to live, to experience a world outside of work. Why not start right here?

The tread of his feet on the stairs was the only sound to puncture the silence. Arousal stirred and her skin prickled at his imagined gaze on her body.

She didn't turn when they were in the bathroom, just stepped into the shower and waited for him to undress and follow. If she hesitated she might lose her nerve. The water ran hot, filling the shower cubicle with steam. She sensed him behind her, heard the door click shut, then turned.

"Let me get that soot off you. My way of saying thank you."

She grabbed the soapy sponge and rhythmically rubbed it across his firm chest, bracing her other hand against his pecs in an attempt to keep herself from sliding. Then she reached up to soap his neck, deliberately grazing her very erect nipples against his skin.

He grabbed the sponge. "My turn. Turn around."

Hardly able to believe she was doing it, she obeyed, letting her head rest back against his chest. *Boy, he's tall. And what's he doing to me?* It felt divine, the soapy sponge sliding over her breasts, making her arch against him and gasp. Then he slid the sponge rhythmically between her legs. It lightly massaged her clit and made her long for the hard erection at her back. She wanted him to put her out of her misery. The anticipation was too much to bear. She tried to twist back round.

"Uh, uh." Drew blocked her, moved her hands up above her head and held them there with his left hand. He continued to massage her until she writhed and bucked against the soapy sponge, letting the wave of pleasure rip through her body, surrendering to his control.

She was living. She was free.

She twisted around, turned on even more at the sight of his dilated pupils and his evident desire.

He bent his head and whispered in her ear. "Now that you're clean, it's time to get dirty." Turning off the shower with one hand, he opened the cubicle door with the other. Then he swept her up into his arms before she had time to even realise what he was doing.

He kicked open the only other door on the landing. The door to her bedroom.

He deposited her onto the bed and grinned.

"Okay?"

She nodded, unable to speak as he knelt down and parted her thighs. Her head swam, overwhelmed with happy hormones and dizzy with desire.

She moaned as he lowered his head between her legs. He teased her with his tongue until she was jerking in his grip.

In the afterglow, it crossed her mind that she didn't know this man and yet there was the undeniable feeling that she did know Drew, that she knew what mattered and she could trust him with her life.

"Your turn?" she gasped, once the waves of pleasure had subsided.

He shook his head, eyes dark with need. "I have to have you

now."

The air felt thick with pheromones and his desire resonated deep within her. A familiar looking foil packet glinted in his hand and he raised an eyebrow, seeking permission. She nodded, feeling free, uninhibited, as though the break with her old life had given her licence to reinvent herself, she let him turn her over and laid her head on her arms, gasping as he entered her from behind. His full length was deep inside, and it felt right. He fitted. In every way that mattered.

She concentrated on the sensations engulfing her body—the illicit thrill, the pure primal pleasure, the ultimate connection between two human beings...and didn't regret her impulsiveness one bit.

As they lay side by side afterwards, spent but content, lightly but unselfconsciously in contact—a foot here, a hand on a hip there—she told him why she had moved to Coombethwaite. "I've been on the legal treadmill since I chose my A-levels at fifteen years old but a colleague of mine, just two years older, died of a brain haemorrhage at her desk. I knew I had to get out and live a little."

"Glad to be of service," Drew answered with a cheeky grin, lightly tracing a line along her collarbone.

Polly glanced at her alarm clock. "It's eleven-forty, almost New Year. And I was worried I wouldn't find anyone to kiss me at midnight!"

He grinned even wider and leapt out of bed. "Come on."

"Where?" Polly was reluctant to leave the cosy intimacy of her bedroom in case the spell broke.

"The village square. Some local bigwig puts on a big firework display and I don't want to miss it."

Chapter Six

What had passed between them had been about more than meeting and reciprocating a physical need. The volume button on Drew's life had been turned up again after lying dormant in mute. His surroundings were vivid, the air fresher and sounds sharper.

He inhaled the scent of wood smoke from next door, and the clean floral notes of Polly's perfume still filled his senses.

They dressed quickly.

Drew grabbed his jacket as they headed out, checking Tabitha couldn't escape first. "This must be a real contrast to London." Drew gestured to the quiet, dimly lit lane leading to the village square. The shadow of Coombe Mountain was just visible once their eyes adjusted to the dark. The estate fields surrounded them but instead of worrying about which fences might need repairing and juggling budgets, he looked forward to the New Year with a lighter heart.

"Just a bit." She grinned. "Not that I saw much of it. What with twenty-hour days and regular all-nighters, I didn't have much of a social life. And colleagues don't make the best friends. After trainee level, the rungs on the career ladder get narrower and narrower."

"Sounds...horrific."

"It wasn't all bad. I earned the money to buy Fox Cottage, after all."

"Do you think you'll find what you're looking for in Coombethwaite?" He reached for her hand, interlacing his fingers through hers as they approached the crowded square.

"I hope so. I'm enjoying New Year's Eve more than I have done in a long time."

"Me too," he said lightly. He would tell her about Rosa another time. Tonight wasn't the night for sad stories and it was true, he was having a good time. "Now don't worry, I promise my lips are sealed about... earlier."

"Thanks." She squeezed his hand.

Groups of friends stood chatting together, clasping their pints. The rest of the crew were coming out of the pub as they approached.

"Hey Drew, did you rescue the old bat's cat?" A stout man in his thirties, face flushed with alcohol, but smiling amiably raised his arm in greeting. He peered closer. "If that's a cat you've got there, I've had more to drink than I thought."

"Just as well you're not on call tonight, Pete. This is Polly, Enid's new neighbour, and you'd better behave yourselves. She's a solicitor!"

He glared at Ken, the fire brigade's newest recruit, who was clearly checking her out. He raised an eyebrow, his body language hopefully shouting "Hand's off!" and pulled Polly closer to his side. She moulded into him in a most satisfactory way. He began to ache for her again.

The village clock chimed and a few streamers were pre-emptively released. Drew turned his face down to Polly's and kissed her. The twins wolf-whistled and, behind his back, he unobtrusively stuck two fingers up at them. When the fireworks started after the twelfth chime, it seemed the whole square was full of people embracing, wishing each other a Happy New Year. Goodwill vibrated on the air and Polly's eyes shone with happiness.

When the last rockets had been fired, no hitch this year thank goodness, he nodded his thanks to the groundsman who'd been responsible for making it all happen according to plan, and the members of the fire crew who'd also gone without a drink to oversee any mishaps. The crowd sang For Auld Lang Syne and he lowered his lips to Polly's ear so she could hear him over the noise.

"Never mind old acquaintances, I'm more concerned with new ones at the moment. What do you say we go home and improve our acquaintance?"

In response she tugged at his hand and they slipped unseen from the crowd down the lane that lead back to Fox Cottage. Flakes of snow filled the sky and drifted gently to the cobbles below. He felt for the bleeper on his belt and realised with relief he was no longer on call.

An awful lot could happen in one night. Rosa had been taken from him one night but tonight Polly had been given to him—an overdue Christmas present lodged in a chimney, just waiting for him to collect.

As if sensing his serious thoughts, Polly reached up and kissed him lightly on the mouth.

"Happy New Year," she whispered.

And somehow he thought that's what it might just turn out to be.

About the author:

Lorraine Wilson currently lives in Wiltshire but has travelled extensively and lived in four continents. From playing amidst Roman ruins as a child in Africa to riding a Sultan's racehorse in the Middle East as a teen she has many experiences to draw on for the stories she has been writing ever since she can remember. She loves reading flirty romances with witty heroines and irresistible heroes and writes both contemporary and historical romances. When she's not writing you'll find her listening to audiobooks while she sews or designs, usually with a terrier or two curled up on her feet.

Books by Lorraine
Confessions of a Chalet Girl

Dear Reader

I hope you've enjoyed this, the first anthology by The Minxes of Romance! We'd love you to visit our blog www.minxesofromance.blogspot.com where you can find out more about the minxes, and from where you can visit all of our individual blogs.

If you've enjoyed the stories, we'd be grateful for a review on Amazon, and if you have any feedback – or suggestions for a topic for our next anthology, just pop over to our blog and leave us a comment!

x The Minxes

Printed in Great Britain
by Amazon.co.uk, Ltd.,
Marston Gate.